WILD
GEESE

WILD GEESE

CAROLINE PIGNAT

Red Deer PRESS

5 4 3 2 1

Published by
Red Deer Press
A Fitzhenry & Whiteside Company
195 Allstate Parkway, Markham
ON L3R 4T8
www.reddeerpress.com

Edited by Peter Carver
Cover design by Alan Cranny
Cover images: photograph of the author's eyes courtesy of Marion Pignat;
remaining images courtesy of Alan Cranny
Text design by Tanya Montini
Printed in Canada

We acknowledge with thanks the Canada Council for the Arts, and the Ontario Arts Council for their support of our publishing program. We acknowledge the financial support of the Government of Canada through the Book Publishing Industry Development Program (BPIDP) for our publishing activities.

 Canada Council **Conseil des Arts**
for the Arts **du Canada**

 ONTARIO ARTS COUNCIL
CONSEIL DES ARTS DE L'ONTARIO

Library and Archives Canada Cataloguing in Publication
Pignat, Caroline
Wild geese / Caroline Pignat.
ISBN 978-0-88995-432-8
1. Grosse Île (Montmagny, Québec)—History—Juvenile fiction.
2. Immigrant children—Ontario—Juvenile fiction. I. Title.
PS8631.I4777W54 2010   jC813'.6   C2010-904508-4

Publisher Cataloging-in-Publication Data (U.S)
Pignat, Caroline.
Wild geese / Caroline Pignat.
[256] p. : cm.
Sequel to Greener Grass.
ISBN: 978-0-88995-432-8 (pbk.)
1. Irish – Canada – Migrations – History – Juvenile fiction. 2. Canada – Emigration and immigration – History – Juvenile fiction. 3. Ireland – Emigration and immigration – History – Juvenile fiction. I. Title.
[Fic] dc22   PZ7.P5463Wi 2010

To Mom and Dad for giving me roots
and for giving me wings.

I love you.

Where are the swift ships flying
Far to the West away?
Why are the women crying
Far to the West away?
Is our dear land infected
That thus o'er her bays neglected
The skiff steals along dejected
While the ships fly far away?

– Thomas D'Arcy McGee

THE CROSSING

CHAPTER ONE

I should be dead by now. Some days I wish I was. My eyes have seen enough sorrow; I just want to close them to its sting. But there is something inside me that pushes on. A heart that beats no matter how battered or broken.

I suppose we all have that desperate determination, all us steerage passengers. Huddled in tattered groups around small cook fires Captain MacDonald allows us to burn on deck, with nothing to our names but the tales we tell, great comfort comes from the warm glow on our faces and the hot tea in our bellies after so many days in the dark hold. And it's only been two weeks. We've another four to go yet. So long. But what choice have we?

Standing, I face the wind gushing over the prow as the ship charges into the gaping black. My inspiration is out there ... somewhere. Mam, Jack, and Annie sail ahead of us on the *Dunbrody* bound for Quebec. Maybe they're standing on their deck, watching this same whittled moon, thinking of me. Or maybe they think I'm long dead. They don't know I'm only days behind them. For all they know, the Lynch lads found me and dragged me to jail for trying to poison Mr Lynch.

The salt air scuffs my cheeks and I breathe it in. Let it scour the places in me where hope has gone stale from long hours in the musty hold.

No. We will find each other. We will be together again. Even when I see nothing but emptiness ahead. I have to believe it. For a glimmer of hope is all I've got.

It boggles the mind to think that the Captain navigates this massive ship by a star's twinkle, or so Mick says. As though Mick knows a lick about sailing. Just because he's working as a sailor for his passage, doesn't mean he knows a blessed thing about the sea. Sure, all he does is scrub decks or get sick over the ship's rail. But with nothing to see but water and sky, maybe the heavens are giving us some direction. It's hard not to think of the storms ahead, the depths below, or the folk left behind, but survival means fixing our eyes on that glimmer as the darkness closes in.

"Douse them fires," a sailor's voice calls as he rings the ship's bell. Though we're let up on deck to cook when the weather's fine, it's time now to return to the hold. I will wait until the last moment to be back in the ship's belly. The night sky spans from horizon to horizon, a dark field lush with stars. I choose a few and commit them to memory, a slipping of sky tucked in my mind for those long, long hours with nothing before me but dirty berth boards.

"Time to go, Kit," Mick says, appearing behind and gently touching my elbow.

I nod. Jealous that he gets to stay. To feel the wind on his face. To have a sailor's hammock and meals for himself, while I have to get stuffed in my berth like a forgotten weed on Lizzie's shelves, uprooted and withering for want of air. I can't look at him. I should be thanking him for bringing me; I wouldn't be here if it weren't for Mick. But on those long days of darkness, when the sea pounds the other side of the planks, hungry to swallow me whole, I huddle in my corner of the hold and cry. I should be praying. But I can't. All I can think is: I wouldn't be here if it weren't for Mick O'Toole.

I dawdle the length of the ship to the hatch. The last one down the wooden steps, I glance back for one more look at the sky, the twinkling sky framed by the hatchway's darkness. Da used to take me to the top of the hill on nights like this, when the fishhook moon hangs from a net of stars. 'Tis as if he is standing here next to me now. *Don't be afraid of the dark, pet. For that's when the stars shine brightest.*

My glimmer of hope is like that, too. I hold it tight. For without it, I'd be utterly lost.

CHAPTER TWO

Old Murph notches another day on the berth post as we settle for the night. But those little scratches just aren't happening fast enough.

"Two weeks already," Murph says with a grin.

Two weeks. It feels like two months since I first came down those stairs into this horrible hold. I remember the terror I felt. Before my eyes could adjust, my nose told me all I needed to know. Without a window or door, other than the hatch at the top of the stairs, the air hung heavy, thick with the stench of fear. With every step, it swallowed me. My heart thudded in my chest. I had to get out. I couldn't stay here another minute.

"Let me through!" I had cried, pressing against the wave of passengers spilling into the hold. "I can't … I have to … let me out!"

Murph saved me that first day. "Are you traveling by yerself, son?" he'd asked. At first, I didn't think he was talking to me. I'd forgotten I'd disguised myself as Kenny O'Toole, Mick's brother, to get on board. 'Twas Mick's idea. Otherwise the Lynch lads would surely have caught me and dragged me back to Wicklow Jail. I am a wanted criminal back home. As the crowd swept me back into the darkness, I remember wondering if a quick hanging would have been better. Some days I still do.

"Name's John Murphy," he'd said. "But everyone calls me Murph." He'd offered me a corner of his berth, and so I'd followed him through the crowd, past the long tables that ran the length of the hold. There were hundreds of us down there, jostling for space in the murky light of a few lanterns. Fights broke out as people claimed their bags were there first, while others scurried like rats eager to shove their bundles in shelves stacked three high, running the length of the ship.

At the farthest corner, in what must have been the very back of the ship, Murph stopped and nodded to the upper shelf.

"That's us here." He'd climbed up and disappeared into the dark. Stepping on the bottom shelf, I had peered after him. 'Twas nothing more than a few bare boards covered with a bit of straw. Six feet square, if that, and only eighteen inches head space.

"We're staying here?" I'd asked. "Aren't these storage shelves?"

"That they are," he'd chuckled. "You'd best be storing yourself up here, lad. The place is filling up quicker than a thimble in a storm."

He'd introduced me to his grandchildren, Joe, a lad about my age, and wee Brigid who was four, as well as Mrs. Ryan, an older woman traveling alone who shared the berth. They were nothing but dim shapes huddled in the darkness. Strangers, really. But God knows where I'd be without them.

"*Only* two weeks?" Joe whines as Murph puts his knife away. Two weeks wasn't even halfway there.

"It feels like we've been in this hold forever," I mumble, lying on my back and staring at the long planks that run the length of the deck, trying to hold on to my scrap of sky.

"Enough of your moaning, now," Murph scolds. "As penance, you've to tell me three things you're glad of at this very moment." He did that every time we bellyached. We'd been doing "penance" a lot lately. "And no repeating," he adds.

"I'm thankful we have this corner berth," Joe starts. "Even if it bloody stinks down here."

"That's awful close to bellyaching, wouldn't you agree, Kenny?"

"Definitely," I say.

"I'm thankful we get to go on deck again soon, I hope," Joe adds. "So I can get away from you lot."

"Bellyache," Brigid and I reply.

"And three," Joe says, "I'm thankful it's so dark in here you can't see me sticking out my tongue at you."

"Nor I at you, Joe," little Brigid adds.

I laugh. "I'm thankful for Brigid's sense of humor."

"And?" Joe teases.

"And I'm thankful for Joe, even if you are a right bellyacher."

"Oh, come on, Grandad. That's a bellyache if I ever heard

one. And besides, that's only two."

"All right then," I stare at the boards above. "I'm thankful for … friends."

"I'm thankful for you, too, Kenny," Joe adds.

"Oh, I wasn't talking about you, Joe," I say.

Joe punches my arm as Murph and Mrs. Ryan chuckle in the shadows.

I can't imagine this trip without them. Lying side by side, all night and most of the day, talking, laughing, listening to them breathe reminds me of home, of sleeping with Annie and Jack in the settle bed or nattering by the fire. It makes being stuck in the hold almost bearable.

"I'm thankful Da's waiting for us in Richmond," Joe says then.

I think of Mam, Annie, and Jack. *Will they wait for me?* My stomach clenches at the thought of never seeing them again.

Brigid twiddles a piece of straw in her fingers. "Mammy and wee Mary were supposed to be coming with us but … the fever … and well, you know …"

Murph rests his hand on the girl's shoulder.

"Yeah," I murmur. "I know."

I know all too well. Famine, disease, loss. Sadly, my story is no different than the hundred others stacked on these berth shelves. I've heard so many these past two weeks. Homes destroyed. Families torn apart. Around the cook fires and in shadowy berths, we talk about our villages, our loved ones, the way it was. We sympathize. But it doesn't change anything. Our stories are what they are. And after a while, we stop telling them.

I close my eyes and try not to think of the deep fathoms, the bottomless sea that churns on the other side of a few creaky boards. I never liked the sea. Not even when Don Kelly treated me and Millie to a ride in his fishing boat last spring. Not being able to swim is probably part of it, but if you ask me, people no more belong on the sea than they do in the sky. Each day I fear we are going to sink to our watery graves.

Twelve months, not even, since I sailed in Don's boat, since my whole family gathered around the hearth. It seems so much longer.

I close my eyes to the ship's darkness and see myself there … home. I can almost feel Annie's weight in my lap, almost hear the knitting needles click in Mam's hands as baby and blanket grew, see the sparkle in Jack's eyes as Da told his tales. "You are the sons and daughters of the kings of Ireland," Da always said.

I believed so many things back then. Da's stories. Mam's faith. And where did it get us? Our home burned to the ground. Our family divided. Mam's spirit broken. Da gone. *Oh, Da.* The thoughts rush at me, dragging me under. Drowning me in their sorrow.

The rumble of conversation dwindles away for the night. Cramped in their berths, every man, woman, and child lies thinking of all they've left behind, fearing the unknown ahead. A few people cry, the cover of shadows their only comfort as the great ship rocks side to side, and I cry with them.

It comes then, warm and strong. A voice in the darkness.

I'm bidding farewell to the land of my youth
and the homes I love so well

In the shadows, Murph rests against the berth post, eyes closed, singing from his heart.

And the mountains so grand round my own native land,
I'm bidding them all farewell.

Somewhere, from the front of the boat, a whistle joins in, then two fiddles from the side, and a bodhran softly beating as our quiet voices unite.

With an aching heart I bid them adieu
for sadly I'm sailing away,
O'er the raging foam-for to seek a home
on the shores of Amerikay.

Music fills the hold and for that moment, fills our hearts with a much-loved sound.

The sound of home.

CHAPTER THREE

"When are they letting us on deck?" Joe asks two days later. "I could eat the legs off that bench. And that's not a bellyache, Grandad. It's a fact."

"I can't say, Joe." Murph glances at the hatch where people are lining up, waiting for the order from Captain MacDonald. He rubs his knee. "But he best be doing it soon. I daresay there's a storm coming."

"Poor old Widow Delaney hasn't long in this world," Mrs. Ryan's voice interrupts as she climbs back into our berth. It takes her a few tries and grunts, but Murph gives her a hand. She glances around and lowers her voice. "Folk are talking. Saying she's red with rash, that she has the fever. Only her son Brian will touch her. But, says I, wasn't Widow Delaney inspected by the doctor just the same as us? Surely to God they wouldn't let a sick woman on board … would they?" She looks to Murph for reassurance, only, he's staring off, deep in thought. No doubt thinking the same as me. Folk can carry the fever for days before the signs show. Any one of us could have brought it on board.

"Has she any swellings in her side?" I ask. "How far has the rash spread?"

"Listen to Doctor Kenny, here," Joe chides, and I realize a young boy like I'm supposed to be shouldn't know about such things.

Mrs. Ryan shrugs and wraps her shawl about her. "I wasn't getting close enough to see."

"Fancy a walk, Kenny?" Murph asks.

I nod.

"You're mad, the pair of you," Joe mutters as he flops onto his back.

We travel the hold, past the bundles and buckets by berth after berth. Many folk have hung ragged blankets or shawls as curtains, making what privacy they can in such cramped quarters, but most call out to Murph as he walks past. I daresay he knows each by name. Finally we reach the Delaneys' berth in the front corner. Widow Delaney lies still under a tattered blanket with a sick bucket nearby. A man sits on the edge of the berth while eyes peer from shadows in the berth above.

"Brian," Murph rests his hand on the man's shoulder. "How's your mother?"

"Resting now," Brian says, nodding at the bit of oatcake beside her. "She won't eat."

As if a woman in her state would.

"She needs water, not food," I murmur, loud enough for Murph to hear.

Back home, Lizzie once showed me what signs to look for if it's fever: sweating, a swelling in the stomach, a rash that doesn't go white when you press against the skin. By the sheen on her face, even in this dim light, I can tell Widow Delaney's hot to the touch. The telltale red speckles travel the inside of her arms. She moans but her eyes stay shut.

"I feel so helpless," Brian says.

"Maybe get her to drink a sup of water," Murph offers.

Taking a few dried sprigs from the small bag Lizzie gave me the day we left Killanamore, I slip them into Murph's hand and whisper in his ear. Murph nods and gives them to Brian. "Here. Steep these in a tea and get her to drink as much as you can. It might help with the pain."

"God bless you, Murph."

"If you need anything," Murph says, nodding the length of the ship, "sure, we're only down the road. 'Tis no distance at all."

"Thanks," Brian says. "Thanks for stopping by."

Murph leads the way back down the other side of the tables, ducking under the web of lines folk tied to the masts. High above deck, those massive poles hold sails that snap in wind and shine in the sun. Yet down below, they bear ragged scraps of shirts and breeches that hang forever wet in the dark, damp hold.

"So tell me, now," he calls over his shoulder. "Where'd you learn about remedies?"

"Back home I often worked for Old Lizzie, gathering roots and whatnot for her tonics. She was the wise woman in our village." I duck under a shawl draped over the drying line. "I wish she was here now. She'd know what to do."

"Well, I daresay you gathered up a bit of her wisdom as you gathered her roots."

"Murph." I stop him and he turns to face me as we stand hidden among the laundry lines. I lower my voice. "'Tis the fever Widow Delaney has."

He stares at the floorboards. "I feared as much. Will she live?"

"Maybe if we were back home, if I had fresh roots and hot broth. Maybe then I could do something, but I don't know how to fight the fever here." The truth of it settles across my shoulders like a cold, wet shawl.

"Is there nothing we can do, then?" Murph asks, both of us knowing he is no longer talking about Widow Delaney.

"I don't know ..."

What would Lizzie say? What would she do?

"Separate the sick. Wash the clothes. Keep the hatch open for fresh air. 'Tisn't much," I say.

"But something, at least." Murph nods. "We'll do what we can and leave the rest in God's hands."

Somehow that doesn't make me feel any better.

CHAPTER FOUR

The queue is barely moving as we wait, cups in hands, in the rations line on deck. We get a cupful of oats and water rations each day, if the weather is fine. With the storm on the horizon, we are anxious to get served before the captain sends us below. The old Scot they call Fergal is doling out the rations, carefully measuring each cup down to the very last drop and oat. Six pints of water per person; 'tis up to each person whether they use it to drink, cook, or wash. Needless to say, most of us are going dirty. I don't mind waiting in the line, though; I'm just glad to be out in the fresh air.

"Is your brother afraid of heights?" Joe asks, shielding his eyes from the sun as he looks up at the sails. I follow his gaze, only to find Mick away up at the second sail, clinging to the mainmast for dear life. What in God's name is he doing now?

"O'Toole!" First Mate Smythe yells from the deck far below. "Get a move on!"

The other three sailors have already shuffled across the footropes and stand waving and yelling at Mick. They can't hoist the sail without a fourth person, but the way Mick has his arms and legs lashed around that mast, the way his shirt flutters wildly in the wind, the way the mast teeters side to side with the rocking of the ship, makes me think he's never letting go.

"Mick!" I yell. "Get down!" He has no business being up there. That fool of a boy will kill himself, he will.

He opens his eyes and turns to the sound of my voice, but a glimpse of Joe and me seems only to spur him onward. Steeling himself, he lets go of the mainmast and lunges for the yard, but his foot slips off the footrope and he drops. His arms catch the yard before he falls to his death, leaving him dangling from the yard as his long legs flail beneath him like two cut ropes. The crowd below gasps and points. I try not to think of the sight of him plummeting into the sea or the sound of him hitting the deck.

His feet flounder for something solid as his arms begin to lose their grip. He can't hang like that for long.

"Good God, O'Toole, if you're trying to kill yourself, save us all the trouble and just walk the plank!" Smythe shouts. "Coyle, help him out!"

"Aye, sir!" the young sailor next to Mick answers and edges over to Mick, whose kicking feet catch Coyle in the shins. Grabbing the back of Mick's trousers, Coyle gives a yank and lifts Mick until his feet find the swaying rope. By the look of Coyle, he's not too happy. He motions to Mick how to hoist the sail by pulling it hand over hand. Mick nods like he knows what Coyle is talking about.

I'd already seen Smythe tear a strip off of Mick for spilling the Cunninghams' chamber pot across the deck last week. Even I knew Mick hadn't his sea legs. He walked like Ned Nowlan coming home from the pub, lurching and listing, stopping every few steps to be sick. Smythe made Mick scrub those planks for hours. If only we'd had the money for two tickets, Mick could have been in the berth with us instead of trying to be someone he's not. Of course, who am I to judge? 'Tis thanks to my warrant that we're both imposters.

"Today, O'Toole!" Smythe yells, as Mick leans over the yard and grips the canvas like the other sailors. Only, on the count of three when they heave the sail, Mick heaves his breakfast. Vomit spills over the yard and down the sail to hit Smythe like a bucket of slops.

"Jaysus, your brother is in for it now," Joe whispers. And don't I know it. For there is Smythe, his face as red as his uniform, both slathered in Mick's hot sick.

"If the climb down doesn't kill him," Joe adds, "Smythe surely will."

"*O'Toole*!" Smythe's voice slices the air like a bloody cutlass. "Get your sorry Irish arse down here … *NOW*!" He turns to the crowd, eyes blazing. "The rest of you back in line or it's back in the hold!"

We lower our gaze and wait our turn. By the time we've gotten our cups of oats and water and settled by the fire, Coyle is lowering Mick to the deck by a rope around his waist. I don't want to see Mick's shame, but there's no missing it.

"O'Toole, I have given you every possible chance," Smythe rants, slapping away the rags a sailor hands him. His pristine uniform is darkened in wet, sticky patches. Porridgey bits and chunks of God knows what stick to his hair and on his shoulders. He points his finger at Mick, who sits where he landed on the vomit-covered deck as though he hasn't the strength to rise. "Every chance! But you can't be learned. I said so to the captain. Just look at you! Are you some kind of idiot? A simpleton, perhaps? Or are you just that pathetic?"

Mick, eyes down, doesn't answer. Years of Lynch's wrath back home had taught him the best reply was none. He'd learned that from his father. And *his* father before that.

"You're no sailor. Not even a man," Smythe sneers. "You'll never amount to anything. Do you hear me?" He pauses. "Do you, you good-for-nothing Irish?"

"Yessir," Mick mumbles.

"Look at me when I'm talking. Stand up when you're being addressed. I'm your commanding officer, damn you!"

Shaking, Mick stands. He's so pale, I worry he might get sick again, but Smythe backhands him across the face and Mick falls back.

"Fetch me the flayed rope," Smythe orders. "This boy needs a lesson."

CHAPTER FIVE

As I jump to my feet, my eyes meet Mick's across the deck. I can't watch this anymore. Back home, I'd run, run up the hill to my special stone and watch the sea until the tide receded, taking all my anger with it. But where can I run now? I'm surrounded by the sea. I've no stones, no tides, no place to go. But I can't stay here.

My feet pound the boards as I bolt to the forbidden aft deck, up the steps, past Lord and Lady Cunningham's quarters, past the ship's wheel 'til I hit the railing and can run no further. My heart pounds in my chest. I want to keep running, to jump over this rail, to go back, back to the way things were before the famine.

But I can't.

"Are you lost?" a voice says from behind. I turn to see Captain MacDonald coming toward me.

"I'm sorry sir, Captain, sir," I mumble. Steerage passengers are not allowed anywhere but the hold and the main deck when called. I wonder if I'll be whipped for trespassing. "I'm Kenny O'Toole and my brother, Mick, well, he vomited on First Mate Smythe and now he's going to be whipped." The words rush out, but before I'm done, Captain MacDonald is heading for the main deck with me in tow.

"What's all this, Smythe?" the captain asks as the sailors part for him.

"It's O'Toole, Captain. The sailor I told you about."

"Yes, well his brother here was just telling me about you."

Smythe glares at me but I meet his eyes. I won't look away. I won't give him that.

"I've sailed for twenty years," the captain continues, taking the rope from Smythe's hands. "Since when is whipping prescribed for seasickness? And look at your uniform and the state of these decks."

"It wasn't me, Captain," Smythe says. A pleading tone seeps

into his voice. "It's him. He—"

Captain MacDonald holds up his hand. "Whose uniform is it?"

"But he—"

"*Whose* uniform?"

"Mine, sir," Smythe admits.

"And whose responsibility is it to run a tight ship, keep the decks clean, and the sailors up to par?" the captain asks, clasping his hands behind his back.

"Mine, sir," Smythe answers.

Lord and Lady Cunningham peer down from the aft deck. Lady Cunningham raises a lace hankie to her nose in disgust. Most ships have rooms for the middle class, though they rarely mixed with the steerage passengers.

"Everything all right, Captain MacDonald?" Lord Cunningham asks.

"Yes, Lord Cunningham. Mr. Smythe is just taking care of it, aren't you, Mr. Smythe?"

"Yes, sir, right away, sir." Smythe turns but the captain leans over.

"For God's sake, man. Go and change your uniform, will

you? You stink to high heaven."

Smythe's eyes bore into mine. He scowls at Mick and heads for his quarters. But this isn't over. Not by any means.

Within minutes, the captain has the sailors back at work. Another sailor joins Coyle to hoist the sail.

"You two," the captain says as they climb down to the deck.

"Aye, sir?" Coyle puffs up like a proud cockerel to be noticed by the captain.

"Get these decks in order."

"Aye, sir." Coyle's lips tighten. He glances at Mick and clenches his jaw before heading for the buckets and brushes. This is going to cost Mick something fierce.

"Ever do any carpentry, Mick?" Captain MacDonald asks.

"No, sir," Mick mumbles. I can tell he's terrified he might be asked to. "I can whittle a stick, but that's all."

The captain strokes the wooden rail. "Every piece of this ship is built to serve a specific purpose. A square peg will never fit in a round hole. Men like Smythe will try to force it, but what good is that? It weakens the structure and damages the peg."

"But that square peg belongs somewhere, doesn't it, Captain?"

I blurt. His words stoke something deep inside me. "It's needed somewhere."

He smiles and nods.

Mick frowns. "So I've to find the hole for a p-peg, Captain, sir ... is that right?"

The captain pats Mick's shoulder. "Just keep searching for your place, lad. And stay close to your brother. He's a sharp one, that Kenny. In the meantime, perhaps you could be of help to our ship's cook. Fergal," he calls to the old Scot sealing the water barrel. "Mick here is going to be your new assistant."

Fergal nods and, reaching into his pocket, tosses Mick a bit of root. "Get that into you, now. I'll no have you wasting my food by pitching it into the sea, nor onto Smythe."

"Ginger," I say, smelling the peppery-sweetness burst from Mick's mouth as he takes a small bite. I remember it from Lizzie's stores. "Calms the stomach."

"Aye, gin*ger-r-r-r*." The "r-r-r" makes Fergal's tongue purr. He grins at me. "I may be in need of two assistants, Captain. Might I call the young lad up from the hold from time to time?"

"Yes, of course," he raises his eyebrow and glances at the

dark clouds on the horizon. "Lash those barrels tight, Fergal.

We're in for a good one."

CHAPTER SIX

The ship heaves violently, knocking Joe off balance. His head thunks the post like a pitched apple but his cursing is lost in a clap of thunder. Rain hammers the decks above our heads and the constant creak of timbers kicks up to a screech as the ship heaves and groans. Brigid and her little friend Alice play under the open hatch, catching the raindrops on their tongues.

"Brigid, pet, come away from there before you catch a chill," Mrs. Ryan calls.

"We'll get her," Joe offers, and I follow him over the berth boards and up a third of the hold to the stairs. The *Erin* dips and lurches to the left, forcing me to grab the table to keep my balance. Light from the swinging lantern above it tumbles the shadows, making my head dizzy.

The ship has never rocked so much. The way she whines in protest as her timbers bend and twist makes me think the next creak will surely end with a snap. A crack in her hull would be the end of her, would be the end of us all.

She tips violently to the right, sending seawater through the hatch into the hold, as though the sailors were tossing it down by the bucket. Brigid and Alice scream, caught in the sudden downpour. "Douse them lanterns!" a sailor calls down the hatch.

Reaching Brigid, I pick her up. She's soaked to the skin and shivering. Joe gets Alice as passengers reluctantly snuff the lanterns' light.

"I'm afraid of the dark," Brigid cries, tightening her arms about my neck as the hold's black swallows us. A dim shaft of light comes down the hatch, the last glimmer in the hold, and I head for it. With Brigid in my arms, I grab the rope handrail for balance and yell up at the shadow of the sailor. "You can't leave us like this, in darkness!"

His face shows in a flash of lightning.

"Mick? Mick is that you?" I call. Brigid's arms clench in the thunder's boom. "Can't we keep a small candle burning? You don't have to tell."

"No, Kit. A fire in the hold would kill us all. 'Tis the captain's orders. I'm sorry." He lifts the hatch door.

"You're not closing that on us, too?" Joe yells from beside me. "You're not leaving us in total darkness!"

Mick hesitates. "Captain's orders," he answers. "I'm sorry."

Joe scurries up the steps to stop him.

"Mick, you can't!" I yell. "No, don't! We—"

The hatch door slams, cutting off all light and words.

In the blackness, I hear Joe pound the hatch. "It's locked! He's locked us in!"

Curse you, Mick, you thunderin' eejit. I'll kill you, I will. How could you do this to us?

To me?

I stand frozen, blinded by darkness and fear as the ship groans and heaves hard to the left.

"The ship is sinking," a man screams, "and we're trapped in it!"

"Christ Almighty," a woman wails. "We're going to die in here!"

Panic spreads through the black hold like a thatch on fire. In the total darkness, people scream and shove, desperate with blind terror as our world tilts.

Brigid's arms cinch in another notch around my neck, making it even harder for me to breathe. Her heart flutters like a bird trapped in her bony chest. Or maybe 'tis my own heart racing. "I've got you, Brigid," I say, squeezing her back. "Joe? Where are you? Joe!" I call in the direction of the hatch, my voice drowned in the mob. The ship pitches forward and drops, rolling hard to the left side, slamming me back against the hull. Trunks, kettles, cudgels, chamber pots, anything and everything not tied down flies about the hold.

"My leg!" someone cries near me. "Jaysus, I think it's broken! God help me!"

Women wail. Children scream. All two hundred feet of the hold is utter chaos in the terrifying dark.

"What do we do, Kenny? What do we do?" Brigid asks. Everything in my body tells me to run, run away, get out. A half-crazed voice wants me to scratch at the hull, to dig free from this watery coffin. I take a deep breath.

"Grab hold of this post!" I finally say, hugging it and getting Brigid to do the same on the other side. We clutch each other's arms around the beam. "It'll save us from getting thrashed about."

"And what if the boat sinks?" Brigid asks. "What if—"

A clang sounds on the other side of the pole and Brigid's grip loosens.

"Brigid?" I shake her slack arms. "Brigid! Answer me!"

But my cries go unanswered, like hundreds more in the darkness.

CHAPTER SEVEN

I don't know how long the storm lasts. It feels like I've been huddled under the hatch steps forever. But I dare not emerge from their cover as the rocking ship pitches pots, buckets, and bodies about the black hold. Brigid lies limp in my arms. Though she's breathing, she doesn't stir. Everything's wet and, in the darkness, I can't tell if she's bleeding or if bones are broken. All I know for sure is that she's alive. We're alive. For now.

The rocking and heaving eventually subside as the storm passes, but the panic in the hold continues as people try to find their bearings, to find their loved ones. When the sailor opens the hatch and tells the injured to come on deck, everyone rushes the stairs for a chance to escape this black hole. Injured or not, we all need convincing that we are indeed still in the land of the living. Brigid and I are the first up. I squint against the dim light of the gray sky. I honestly thought I'd never see it again.

Fergal takes her from me as I reach the top step. "She hit her head, I think," I say as he lays her on the deck by the rail. "I'm not sure if anything else is broken."

As the crowd of people spills out behind us, I keep an eye out for my berth-mates, pray they're safe. Finally, I see Murph coming towards us. He's leaning on Mrs. Ryan and Joe. By the way Murph moves, I can tell his right leg is giving a lot of pain, but he's walking on it. At least it isn't broken.

"She's all right," Fergal says, checking Brigid's eyes. There's no doctor on board, but Fergal takes charge. "Got a good clatter in the head, though."

"Brigid, love." Murph winces as he lowers himself by his granddaughter. "Wake up now, pet. Open your eyes."

"I don't know what hit her." I stroke the welt on the side of her temple. "Whatever it was, it hit her hard."

Fergal takes a vial out of a medical bag and, uncorking it,

waves it under Brigid's nose.

She coughs. "Mammy?" she moans and starts crying.

"She'll be all right, soon," Fergal says. "I'll get you something for her head. Try and keep her talking."

"Kit!" Mick yells, running over to me through the crowd of broken and bloodied passengers spilling onto the deck.

Did he just call me Kit? Posing as his brother was his bright idea, yet, here he is, this eejit, yelling, "Kit!" at the top of his lungs in front of the whole bloody ship.

"You're bleeding!" He grips my arms and looks me over. "Jaysus! Are you hurt? Are you all right?"

"What do you care?" I snap, thrashing free of him.

"I was so worried about you," he says. "I'd never forgive myself if anything ever happened to you."

"You closed the damned hatch on me. On us," I add as Joe joins me.

"I had to," Mick says, avoiding Joe's glare. "If the hold filled with water, the ship would surely sink. I was just following orders."

"Following orders? Why is it that the first time you do your bloody job right, 'tis to lock me in the hold?" I can't even look at him. I want to throttle him. "Just stay away from me."

"Kit," he grabs my arm again as I turn to leave, but Joe shoves him hard, knocking him back.

"Forget about him, Kenny," Joe says, turning his back on Mick. "Your brow is a right mess. It needs looking after."

I don't need my cut checked. It may be bleeding a lot, for face wounds do, but I know 'tisn't deep. Still, I let Joe lead me. It irritates Mick to the point that he storms off, and that is fine by me.

"What did he call you? Kit?" Joe asks as we cross the deck.

"Family nickname," I mutter, hoping he'll buy it. Confusion furrows his forehead. It's hard enough to keep secrets from my friends without Mick's big gob interfering.

"Why does he—"

I swoon, forcing a subject change.

"Easy now." He guides me to sit by Murph as we wait for Fergal's examination.

"Go easy on Mick," Murph's voice rumbles beside me. I know his old eyes have been watching the whole thing. "It seems to me that you're all he's got."

"I didn't ask to be." I say. But 'tis true. I am all he has. And

God help me, that lad is going to be the death of me if this trip doesn't kill me first.

Brian Delaney slumps beside us and puts his head in his hands. "She's gone, Mam's gone," he says, wiping his eyes. "She passed away during the storm."

"God rest her soul," Murph answers.

"I suppose the storm was too much for her to handle in her weakened state," Brian adds, and we nod, Murph and I. For we dare not speak the truth of it.

Murph tries to stand. "I'll let the captain know, shall I? We should bury her as soon as possible." But he groans with the pain in his leg and I offer to go instead.

"Bury her? Sure, where would we find a cemetery out here?" Brian asks as his eyes scan the dark horizon, and then he knows. "You don't mean to throw her overboard? Not my mother, and that not even holy ground."

"We'll bury her at sea, son," Murph says. "'Tis all God's creation and that makes it holy enough."

Brian clenches his jaw and nods. For what choice has he?

Avoiding Smythe, who barks orders in the front of the ship,

and Coyle, who scowls at me as I walk by, I find the captain by the mainmast where he's giving orders to two sailors armed with carpentry tools. It looks like the *Erin* suffered some injuries from the storm as well. The tip of the yard, tangled in its ropes, swings like a dead convict. A jagged sail drapes down the mast. I wonder how serious the wound is in seaman's terms. By the captain's worried look, it seems bad enough, but his eyes soften when he sees me.

"Young O'Toole, isn't it?"

I nod. "Captain, sir, Mr. Murphy asked me to tell you that Widow Delaney, God rest her soul, passed during the storm."

He turns his attention back to the torn sail and motions for the sailors to start climbing. A corpse can wait. "We'll just finish up our repairs and I'll have the crew see to the burial."

"Well, sir, it's just that," I say, "Mr. Murphy believes she died of the fever."

Even though I lower my voice on it, the last word jolts him to a stop. He calls for Fergal and talks to him in hushed tones as they glance at the rows of injured passengers lining the decks. The captain orders the sailors to leave the sails. Half he sends to fetch the body, the rest are to sluice and scrub the hold while everyone is on deck.

"Do any others have it?" the Captain asks Fergal. I notice he avoids the word as though it carries the disease itself.

Fergal shakes his head. "I could check them now as I examine their storm injuries. They'd be none the wiser."

Captain MacDonald nods. "Good. No sense in alarming them any further." He turns to me, rests his hand on my shoulder. "Will you give Fergal a hand, lad? He'll tell you what to look for."

But I know well enough.

CHAPTER EIGHT

"Kenny, I could use a hand here," Fergal calls. I turn to join him, only to find Coyle's massive frame blocking me. Two buckets full of water hang heavy from his hands and a scowl weighs down his face.

"The lads tell me that washing below decks was your bright idea." I can tell he doesn't think it all that bright. He steps in closer. "Now, tell me, will you, why I always get stuck cleaning up? It seems to me that these O'*Fool* brothers are causing me a lot of grief. I'm going to have to do something about that."

I'm glad his hands are busy gripping the buckets and not my neck.

"Come on then, Kenny," Fergal calls. I step to the side, but Coyle rams me with his thick shoulder as he passes, knocking me to the ground.

"Mind yourself, O'Fool," he says, walking past and spilling water from his bucket on me. "You wouldn't want to get hurt in an *accident* now, would you?"

I try not to think about all the accidents that could happen out here in the middle of nowhere: the long drop from the yard arm, the weight of ten barrels crushing the life out of me, being tossed overboard. Coyle grins as though reading my very thoughts. I used to think this ship huge, as long as seven cottages end to end, but now it seems tiny. I'd best be keeping out of Coyle's way, but that's as good as telling fish in a bucket to mind the cat's claws.

Still shaking, I join Fergal at Murph's side. Poor oul' Murph. His knee is badly bruised. Sprained, I'd say. Thankfully, it doesn't seem out of joint or broken. Still, the rum Fergal gives him doesn't ease Murph's pain. He's as pale as his bandages by the time Fergal and I finish splinting the leg.

"Your Lizzie would be proud," Murph says, forcing a smile.

"Stay off it and it'll heal straight and true," I add, using

Lizzie's words. "A few weeks, at least."

"That means stay put," Joe says. "You're not to be gallivanting from one end of the ship to another. Let your friends come see you for a change." I can tell he's worried about the old man. We both are.

"Yes, mammy," Murph says, coaxing our smiles.

Brigid rests in Mrs. Ryan's arms with a cold rag on her head. I check both of them for signs of rash or fever, relieved to find neither.

For the next two hours, Fergal and I make our way from one bruised face to another. Considering the battering we all took in the hold, the injuries aren't too bad. Cuts, gashes, bruises, and a few broken limbs. But even they seem mild when you think of what could have happened. And thanks be to God, no sign of the fever.

"There you go, pet," I say, putting a little girl's arm in a sling around her neck. I tuck her rag doll in with it. "Look at that. A wee hammock of her own." The girl's smile reminds me of Annie's. I wonder how they fared during the storm.

Dear God, I hope they're safe.

Standing, I wipe the back of my hand against my forehead,

careful not to open my cut. My eyes sting and my head aches, probably from whatever left that gash across it. The girl sings her doll a lullaby. She even sounds like Annie. I can't stop staring at her.

"I'm sure they're fine," Mick says quietly. I hadn't noticed him come up behind me. "Your family is strong, Kit. Like you." He puts a cup in my hand and a piece of oatcake in the other. Before I can get any words past the lump in my throat, he's gone.

I sip the cool water, amazed at my thirst, even more amazed that Mick knew it before I did myself.

"Anything?" Fergal asks, as he joins me.

"No. You?"

He shakes his head and glances up at the splintered yard arm and the torn sail.

"Can we sail without it?" I ask.

"Aye," he says, "but it will take us longer. Maybe a week, depending on the winds." Seeing my worry, he tries to reassure me. "With smaller rations of water and food, we'll be fine."

But I wasn't thinking about food. More days meant I'd more chance of being found by Coyle and less chance of finding my family. They didn't even know I was coming. If they went on into Canada without me, how would I ever find them?

Captain MacDonald doesn't waste any time. That evening, he gathers us for Widow Delaney's burial. Two sailors carry what looks like a long scrap of rolled sail sewn up the middle.

"What's that, Grandad?" Brigid asks.

"Mrs. Delaney's remains, God rest her," he whispers.

"Why is she so heavy?" Brigid says. I wonder about that myself, for she was a small woman. The sailors lay the shroud on a long plank leading up to the door in the railing.

"They put stones inside the shroud before they sew it," he whispers, "... to make it sink," he adds before she can ask.

The very thought makes me shudder.

A sailor opens the gate.

"Stones?" Brigid continues. "Now where would they find stones here?"

Murph silently rests his hand on her shoulder as she frowns, caught up in the mystery. She doesn't realize the crew must have packed stones and shrouds for burials at sea. Doesn't know there's fever on board. And, thankfully, doesn't comprehend that any one of us could be next.

With the storm over and the clouds gone, the night sky seems as deep and dark as the sea. And we, but a speck in the midst of them. The moon is near full tonight and Captain MacDonald needs no lantern to read from his prayer book. After a few psalms, he invites Brian Delaney to speak.

"She had a heart of gold, she did," Brian says, his chin trembling. "Even in the darkest days, she'd never see another soul going without." He pauses. His young son takes his hand and Brian squeezes it. "God rest you, Mother."

Someone plays a lament on the tin whistle. I can't help thinking a burial at sea isn't right. 'Tis disrespectful, no matter how many prayers Captain MacDonald reads, nor how fondly Brian speaks. 'Tisn't because we haven't a priest, though that be bad enough. Nor is it because each one of us worries it might be us lying there. It just feels wrong. Even at the worst of the famine, many folk were buried back home with neither priest nor coffin. But buried they were. Laid to rest. And most importantly, laid to rest back home. How can you go to your eternal rest in the sea, a thing forever in motion? Poor Widow Delaney. In all her days, I'll bet she never would have imagined this sort of grave. She must have assumed she'd be laid next to Mr. Delaney in the village cemetery. I shiver at the thought, realizing that I'd not be buried in Wicklow, either. Who knows where my bones will rest now, if they rest at all?

Captain MacDonald nods. A sailor lifts one end of the plank and Widow Delaney's body slowly slides toward the hole in the ship's rail. And then, just like that, she is gone. Dropped overboard like a sack of dirt.

I run to the side, barely able to see the white shroud sink into the black waters as the ship continues on without her. Leaving her behind, with nothing to mark her passing but a splash and the mournful toll of the ship's bell. White-streaked wake disappears in the dark sea behind as though none of us were ever there at all.

The sailors close the doorway. The same one we entered when we boarded all those weeks ago. I hope to God when it comes time for me to go through that door again, 'tis on my own two feet.

CHAPTER NINE

"We're slow going these days, aren't we?" Joe asks.

Murph nods, leaning his weight on the rail as we stare out at the glittering sea. On the mast above the broken yard arm waves a white flag with a red x, a signal for help. Our sail is patched, but the yard needs fixing. Maybe the ship behind has what we need.

It amazes me how quickly that ship gains on us. She's only been a crumb on the horizon since we left Ireland a few weeks ago, but I can clearly see her sails now.

Joe's stomach rumbles. "Is it just me, or is Fergal right cheap with the rations these days?"

'Tis true. Fergal had to cut back on the food to make it last.

Who knows how long we might be at sea now? Joe isn't the only one complaining. Just yesterday, I'd heard folk asking Murph to have a word with the captain. He said he would. But Murph knows as well as I do that you can't get blood from a stone, nor food from an empty barrel. He didn't mention that we might be at sea even longer than expected or, worse yet, run out of food. As much as we complain, Fergal's rationing might very well save us.

"There's no satisfying a growing lad," Murph chides. "You've a hollow leg, Joe. Sure, I'm stuffed." He pats his stomach, which we all know is empty.

"Me, too." I grin. "I couldn't eat another bite."

Joe scowls at us. "All I know is that I'm so hungry I could eat the arse off a low-flying gull."

"Ah, then you must have *two* hollow legs," Murph teases.

"And a hollow head, to be sure," I add, ducking to avoid his half-hearted punch. He tries to catch me as I run around the mast and taunt him from one side and then the other. "Come on then, Joe. Is that the best you've got? You slug!"

He laughs and lunges after me.

"Kenny!" Mick calls from where he stands, as rigid as a

rowan trunk. He glances at Joe, his eyes like two poison berries in the shadows of his face. He looks at me, then, "Fergal needs us."

I've done nothing wrong, yet I feel as though I've been scolded.

"I don't think your brother likes me," Joe mutters as Mick turns and walks away.

"Well, I like you well enough, Joe," I say loudly. "No matter what my *brother* thinks. I choose my own friends."

Mick's shoulders hunch with the weight of it. And rightly so. Who does he think he is, telling me who I can and can't befriend? Mick isn't even my *real* brother.

"Fergal wants us to move this barrel back into the storage," Mick says when I catch up. He won't look at me. "You take this end; it's lighter."

Up close I see his face isn't shadowed but bruised, like a rotten apple. "Mick! What in God's name happened to your face?"

He shrugs. "I had an accident."

Mick always has some new cut or scrape, for he's forever tripping over his own two feet, but that fresh black eye was no accident. Or rather, it was a Coyle kind of *accident*.

I'd done my best avoiding Coyle these past few days. But obviously Mick wasn't as lucky. Or as smart.

"What in the hell are you thinking, Mick?" I scold him. But someone had to tell him to smarten up before he got himself killed. "You don't stand a chance against Coyle. He'll tear you to bits."

He doesn't say anything as he lifts his end of the barrel. We grunt and stagger with the weight of it as we carry it along the aft deck.

"Hide from him. Run away," I continue.

"Like a bilge rat? Am I to cower in the corners?" His intensity surprises me. Mick's never been one to fight back. What has gotten into him?

"Yes," I say. "If that's what it takes. Be a rat. They're good at hiding. You're no good to anybody if you're dead."

He clenches his jaw and says no more about it. He knows I'm right.

We reach a set of the stairs at the far end of the ship. Mick turns and bears the weight of the barrel's bottom as I guide him down from the top. A few doors line the narrow hallway. The last one is open and we enter into a small storage room packed with supplies. The tiny room is stocked with barrels and crates. Long ropes sit neatly coiled on a few lids, and bundles of dried goods swing from the rafters. Had I known we had this much food, I wouldn't have worried. Still, the way Fergal frowns as he tallies his list makes me think all this may not be enough.

"Set that down over there." Fergal nods at the far corner. By my guess, my berth is just on the other side of the wall.

Something furry bumps my foot, scraping its nails on my skin as it scurries past. I scream and drop the barrel.

"Curse ye, ye hairy bastard!" Fergal yells, grabbing a nearby broom and smacking the floor as he runs around the barrels. I've never seen him move so fast. He slams the boards with each word. "Wee! Sleekit! Cowrin'! Beastie!"

'Tisn't English, but I get the gist just the same.

"Mick," Fergal says, winded from the attack, "fetch the traps from the galley, would you?" Mick leaves as Fergal raves on. "No rat is getting any of my stores. Do you hear that, you wee beastie?" He shakes his fist in the air. "A battle to the death!"

'Twould have been funny if it weren't so true. I'd seen enough people starve to death to know the difference a handful of oats can make.

My foot stings and I move into the lantern's light to inspect it. Three red slashes slice the top where the rat had scrabbled across. Blood puddles between my toes leaving red footprints on the worn boards.

"Sit, sit," Fergal urges, and I hop on a nearby barrel as he takes a closer look. "Ach, 'tis deep. It got you good. That needs to be cleaned proper. Stay here while I get my bandages."

We both know the dangers of dirty rats. Horrible creatures. God knows what filth is on its nails.

Fergal's footsteps thump up the stairs, leaving me alone on the barrel listening to the creak and groan of the ship, a sound as familiar to me now as my own heartbeat. Something moves in the corner. Something big.

What sized rat could make that sound?

"Achoo!"

That's no rat.

I hobble around to the barrels in the farthest corner. It came from here. A coiled rope hangs over the lid of one barrel, spilling on the floor. Even I know no sailor would ever leave a rope like that, not on Smythe's watch. And the lid itself isn't on straight. Surely Fergal would not have left it like that. I slide the lid to the side, half-fearing I'll come face to face with a dog-sized, hungry rat inside. Only it isn't a rat. It's a boy about my age, sitting cross-legged in the bottom of the barrel.

"Please … don't tell," he whispers. The whites of his eyes shine from the darkness like two moons.

"Why are you in here?" I ask, though the answer's clear enough. The boy's a stowaway. I glance over my shoulder. Fergal will be back any second. After seeing how he handled the rat, I can only imagine what he'd do to this lad. "Who are you?"

He can tell by my clothes, I'm no sailor. But I can turn him in just the same. He considers for a moment and then whispers, "I'm Billy."

"Do you know what they do to stowaways, Billy?"

His trembling tells me he has some idea.

"Please … I'll do anything you want. Just promise me you won't turn me in."

I stand, lid in hand, wondering what they might do to the one stowing a stowaway. Fergal's footsteps knock the stairs.

"All right, I promise. I won't tell a soul."

He smiles in relief as I close the lid. After piling the rope on top, I manage to hobble back to my barrel just as Fergal enters with a bucket of water and a bandage.

"Here we go," he says, taking my foot in hand. He washes it well and binds it tight.

Fergal has a good heart, I know that, but I also know how he is about rationing food. I look over his shoulder at the bloody footprints leading to and from Billy's barrel. Some help I am. Why don't I just put a sign over it saying *stowaway*?

What if they find him? What would they do to him? How did he even get in here? My mind skips like a stone. 'Tis a water barrel; did he empty it? Will one less barrel of water or one more hungry mouth really make all that difference?

Yes. I think. *Yes, it will*. The truth sinks and settles in the bottom of my stomach.

"Here are the traps," Mick says, entering the storeroom with some wild-looking contraptions. Fergal tells him to set them in the corners.

"I thought rats were good at hiding," Mick says.

"Aye," Fergal says. "He can run, he can hide, but he can be sure I'll find him in the end. Ye hear that, wee beastie? A rat on my ship is as good as dead!"

CHAPTER TEN

The rough weather meant another long stint in the hold. Though 'tis only three or four of Murph's notches, it seems like ages since I've seen the sky. Captain MacDonald said it was for our safety. One can tell he hasn't been down in the hold for a visit. But eventually, the rough seas let up and we are let out.

"A nasty bit of a cold," Murph says, as he blows his nose and hobbles to our small cook fire on deck. "Nothing a bit of fresh air won't fix."

Several folk are suffering from one illness or another. Some are sick from the rocking of the ship; others have colds from the hold's damp and night's chill. I daresay there's lice and fleas in every berth by now. Mrs. Ryan grunts as she sits on deck beside Brigid, who pours her a cup of tea.

Despite the chance to be on deck, even for a short while before the coming storm, Brian Delaney takes two extra helpings back into the hold. None of us speak about his mother or Pat and Danny, his youngest boys. They fell ill a few days back and aren't even able to make it up the stairs. None of us wants to say the unspeakable. That they might have the fever. That it might be lurking in the hold. That we might be next. So we talk of weather, trying to ignore the fear gnawing at our empty bellies.

"She's close now," Murph says, nodding to the back ship behind us. "Only a day or two away, at most."

He's trying to change the subject. To give us hope. But somehow, I don't feel any better.

"Kenny, lad," Fergal calls from where he is carefully measuring cups of oats as Mick doles cups of water. I join them and he hands me the key. "Fetch the sack of rice from the storeroom. This last barrel of oats is near done."

My eyes widen at the words "last barrel."

"Don't worry, we've rice and wheat flour, yet. I can work

miracles, just you see," he winks at me.

I didn't tell anyone about Billy. A promise is a promise. Besides, I'm a runaway criminal, a girl bearing a dead boy's name. Who am I to judge Billy? Surely that's the pot calling the kettle black. At any rate, the fewer who know about him the better. I haven't been to the storeroom since I found him there, but Billy survived this long on his own. At least he has food. Our food. I pray he isn't taking much. Fergal may be able to work miracles, but even the Lord Jesus Christ himself needed two fish and five loaves to get started.

I unlock the storeroom door and light the lantern. "Billy," I whisper. "It's me, Ki- Kenny."

Nothing.

"Billy?" I whisper a bit louder, but there is no reply. Careful not to tread on any rat traps, I find Billy's barrel and lift the lid, afraid I might find a corpse in the bottom. But it's empty.

Thank God.

Relief washes over me. *He's not dead. Just gone.*

But relief soon gives way to panic. *Gone? Gone where? Has he been found?*

Fergal's stories run through my mind, stories of stowaways getting whipped, or worse, keelhauled, tied with a rope and dragged underwater from one side of the ship to the other. I shudder.

"Billy!" I whisper more forcefully. "Come out!"

"Looking for someone?" The voice cuts the air like a clap of thunder, making me jump. It isn't Billy's, that's for sure. But I know the voice. I'd trained myself these past few weeks to bolt at its sound—only, down here there is nowhere to run. I turn to find Coyle blocking the exit like a thick-planked door.

"No." My mind races. "I was just—just checking the barrels."

"Then who's Billy?" Coyle raises his eyebrow and looks around.

Visions of keelhauling flash before my eyes. I can almost feel the rope around my wrists, the burn of the seawater in my lungs. "Oh, Billy? Billy's a rat. Just a rat I named."

Coyle enters the room and swipes an apple from the Cunninghams' stores. He walks past me, searching behind the barrels. Finding nothing, he sits on one and eats the apple.

"Why are you down here?" Coyle asks, suspicious.

"Fergal sent me for rice." My eyes dart around for the bag and I grab it. I pray to God Billy has the sense to stay hidden, wherever he is. I head for the doorway but Coyle jumps into my path.

"I have to go, Coyle," I say. "Fergal's waiting and there's a storm coming."

Thunder rumbles overhead.

"Oh, there's a storm coming all right, O'*Fool*." Coyle steps forward and crunches into his apple, juice from it splattering on my cheek. "I've had nothing but troubles since you and your idiot brother set foot on this ship. You O'Fools are bad luck." He nods with his realization and tosses the apple core. "Bad luck through and through. We can't have that. Not on a ship. Sailors can't abide any kind of bad luck."

I step back. "L-leave me alone, Coyle."

"*Leave me alone, Coyle*," he mimics. "Christ, you sound like a whiny girl."

Panic ripples through me as I consider what might happen if he found out I was a girl.

"I have to bring the rice ..." I clutch it to my chest, "... the storm ..."

Coyle's eyes light up. "Oh, accidents happen all the time in a storm. A clumsy passenger might fall overboard. Nobody'd suspect a thing. And even if they did, Smythe would probably thank me."

He flicks his wrist and, with a click, the knife's blade catches the lantern's light.

He's going to kill me. Gut me like a fish and toss me into the sea.

With a groan, the ship tilts, sending me back against the barrels. But Coyle is as steady as ever. He jabs toward my side and I turn, protecting myself with the rice bag. Coyle's blade slashes, spilling rice from the bag's gaping wound, leaving me with nothing but a tattered sack and an empty prayer.

God help me!

A movement just over Coyle's shoulder catches my eye.

"Billy!" I blurt, knowing he'll be next. The fool is standing atop a barrel, holding a crate overhead.

Coyle turns slightly to catch a glimpse and, instead, catches a crate to the head. It smashes over him and he falls like a sack of flour, setting off a rat trap as he tumbles to the floor.

"Sweet mother in heaven! What have you done?" I say, near breathless.

"You're welcome." Billy smiles, hopping off the barrel to admire his work. Coyle lies in a heap among the rice and splinters. His right hand is caught in a rat trap and blood trickles from a cut over his brow.

"Cor, he's a big'un, ain't he?" Billy brags, as though he's just landed himself a cod.

"Big? He's a bloody ape!" I run my hand through my hair, taking in the mess at my feet. "Jaysus, I'm in for it now."

Crate bits slide along the floor as the ship rocks. Picking up a stick, Billy pokes Coyle. "Do you think he's dead?"

A red stain spreads on Coyle's shirt from his dripping brow.

I lean in. "He's breathing." I didn't know if this was good or bad news. "He'll have a sore head and worse temper when he wakes. Did he see you?"

"I don't think so. I'm not sure; he may have." Billy shrugs.

"Where's that rice, Kenny?" Fergal's voice calls from up the stairs. "The storm is close upon us."

"Tell him there's been an accident. Tell him a stack of crates shifted and fell on Coyle," Billy whispers.

Coyle groans.

"But what about you?" I ask.

"Me?" He puffs up his chest. "Billy Farrell can take care of himself."

I look toward the stairs, unsure. But when I turn back, he is gone.

"Did you hear me, lad?" Fergal stomps down the stairs.

"Fergal! Come quick, there's been an accident!" I call as the old man rounds the corner and takes in the scene: the smashed wood, the rice, and the body sprawled in the midst of it all. "A crate fell on him."

"A crate, eh?" Fergal picks up the slashed bag. "You don't say."

CHAPTER ELEVEN

The knife. The slashed rice bag. Coyle's run-ins with Mick. Fergal is no fool. He knows what happened well enough. I can tell he's wondering how a spit of a "lad" like me could take down someone like Coyle. I'm not giving him any answers but I am grateful that he doesn't ask too many questions.

"I knew you had it in you," Fergal says, bandaging the still unconscious Coyle's head. "I told Mick you could fend for yourself. You do a better job of it than Mick, at any rate. Hasn't he the shiner to prove it?"

"What do you mean?"

"Coyle is forever goading Mick. Mick usually ignores his

tauntings, but when Coyle threatened he'd hurt you, well, that was it. That was when Mick fought back. Or tried to. Coyle near killed him with that one punch."

"The idiot!" I say, cursing Mick under my breath. "He should know better."

Fergal slowly opens the rat trap from Coyle's hand. I could tell by the look, the three fingers were snapped.

"You can't blame a lad for protecting his own," he says.

"I am *not* his own," I blurt, forgetting Fergal saw us as brothers. "I mean, I'm my own person." I pull on Coyle's broken fingers, straightening them for Fergal to splint. He takes a bit of stick from the broken crate and binds the three together against it. Part of me wants to set them crooked.

"Right you are," Fergal answers. "And Coyle here won't be punching much with this mangled hand. Still, would you talk to your brother, Kenny? Before he gets himself killed?"

"Oh, I'll talk to him," I say.

Two sailors carry Coyle to his hammock. Fergal says he might suffer from memory loss. I hope he does. Maybe he will forget about picking on Mick and me, not to mention forget about seeing Billy Farrell. If Coyle remembers Billy, Billy's days on this ship are numbered.

A sailor stands at the far side of the aft deck, waving a flag in each hand, his stiff arms moving like the hands on a clock.

"What's he doing?" I ask.

"Signaling the *Wandsworth*," Fergal says. "Probably asking if they've a yard pole for our repairs."

The *Wandsworth* isn't far behind us now. I can almost see the face of the sailor waving signal flags in reply from its prow.

"You'd best be heading to the hold now," Fergal says, glancing up at the darkened sky as we reach the deck. "Storm's coming." I'm surprised he let me off easy, considering the state of the storage room. "And … Kenny?"

I turn.

"Ye may get your sorry self back here after the storm. That storage room isn't going to tidy itself."

"Yessir."

The storm hits hard but we are ready this time. We learned our lesson from the first one. Everything is tied down or safely stowed as we ride the churning sea, climbing peaks and crests as high as any mountain before the terrible fall into the valley on the other side. Each drop punches my gut. Each twist spins my brain. Wave after wave. Joe and I lie in our berth, side by side in the unlit hold, bumped and tossed by the pitching and rolling of the ship. Thunder claps and whining timbers drown out the sounds of passengers crying, praying, or being sick into buckets.

"Kenny," Joe whispers in the dark beside me. "I'm afraid. I don't want to die."

"Don't think about it, Joe," I say. For that was what Da used to tell me when I'd have my awful nightmares back home. "Use your imagination and think of something else."

That advice got me through so much this long year as I lived through those very nightmares.

"Close your eyes," I continue, "and think of lying on the hillside with the sun on your face."

The ship lurches and we bounce in our berth. A woman screams.

"Jaysus, I can't!" Joe says in a panic. "As much as my mind is telling me, my body doesn't believe it. No hillside feels like this!"

"A wagon, then," I say, for our berth boards do feel like a wagon bed beneath us. "We're in the back of the wagon watching the clouds. Da is taking us into town." I speak quickly to calm him. To calm myself. "Today's the May Day Fair. There's Ned Nowlan, leading his sheep. Howiya Ned! And there's Will Hyland, carrying the basket of wool. He'll be playing his bodhran at the dance tonight. Can't you just smell the apple blossoms?"

The ship pitches again.

"'Tis a right bumpy road," Joe says. "I'm bounced around back here like a load of loose logs. Does he always take this way?"

I smile. "Ah, but this way has the best view. Can you see it?"

I feel him relax beside me.

"I can," he says.

"Describe it, Joe."

And so he does. In the middle of a wide ocean, at the height of the storm, in the bottom of a boat over depths beneath us, we escape, Joe and I, to a winding road on the way to the fair with my Da.

CHAPTER TWELVE

Hours later, the seas calm. There are a few injuries, but nothing compared to the first storm we weathered. The captain allows us back on deck and the crowd lines up at the steps, eager to be free from the smelly hold. I hang back to help Murph up the stairs once everyone's gone. Everyone but the Delaneys.

"Can you bring me up to see how Brian's faring?" Murph asks. I'm in no rush to clean the storage room. Knowing Fergal, he'll have me picking up that rice, grain by bloody grain.

Murph leans on my shoulder and I bear the weight, sparing his bad leg as we wander up the stuffy hold past the emptied berths.

"Did you know they carry lumber on the trip back?" Murph says. "My brother's a shantyman. He cuts the trees they float down the river to Quebec. Them berths come out and this whole hold is loaded with logs." He waves his free arm, taking in the length of the ship. "Imagine that, Kenny. A fleet of forests crossing the ocean, headed for England."

I can well imagine, but it pains me to think on it.

"My village is Killanamore," I say. "Do you know what that means?"

"*Coill Anam Mór*," he says, easily slipping into Gaelic. "Forest of great soul."

I nod.

"Had you a great forest there, then?"

I laugh. "If you call a few scrubs and groves a forest. I asked Da about that once and he told me that long, long ago the hills were thick with woods. The woods of myth and legend."

"Home of the Fianna," Murph says, with a smile. "Those are my favorite tales, too."

"Da once said that the English had come and stripped our forests of wood. Taken what they wanted. Being only little when he told me, I said they should have asked us first."

"What do you think now?" he asks.

"Now I know. There is no asking, only taking. The rich can clear wherever they want of wood. Or people." My eyes travel the span of the hold, the row upon row of empty berths. I can imagine the great Canadian logs filling the length and width of this ship's belly. "And here we are … shipped in the very same hold. We have no more say than those stripped logs." I pause. "Come to think of it, the logs are probably worth more to them."

Murph says nothing. He knows I'm right. The truth of it chokes me, makes my eyes water. I roughly rub at them and clear my throat. I could well imagine what Joe would say if he were here to see me so emotional.

If Murph knows I'm crying, he doesn't let on. "*Anam Mór*. Great Soul. It lives on in every seed." He pauses, lets me chew on that, just like Mam feeding Annie as a babe, one sup at a time. "Uprooted, cut down, stripped—those in power do what they like. But know this, Kenny," he continues, "hear me, now. *Anam Mór*, great soul—*that* can never be taken from us. 'Tis in here." He taps his finger over his heart. "We carry the seed of every story ever told and all the ones we've yet to tell."

"Sure, what stories have I to tell?" I ask. For, if anyone knows any story worth knowing, 'tis Murph.

"Why, the ones you have yet to live," he chuckles. "And knowing you, lad, I bet 'twill be grand, rip-roaring adventures."

He pats my back as we continue up the hold. I notice he isn't limping all that much, and I wonder who is helping who.

"Do you smell that?" Murph whispers, as we approach the Delaneys' berth where Brian watches over his children.

"I'd rather not," I mumble, for I well know the stink of fear, of unwashed bodies, of tumbled sick buckets. But a quick sniff makes my stomach sink.

I'd know that reek anywhere, for I'd smelled it enough times those long months back home. It wafted from the workhouses and funeral carts, it lingered on Lizzie's clothes after her long days of house calls.

Pat and Danny Delaney lie side by each in their berth a few feet away where their father watches over them. I don't have to see the boys' rashes and swellings, don't have to touch their burning foreheads to know. The very air drapes around them, heavy with sick and rot.

"Yes," I say, though every ounce of me wishes I didn't. "I smell it, too."

The smell of the fever.

CHAPTER THIRTEEN

Fergal and Mick sweep the storeroom. Thanks to the storm, the mess of wood and rice has been flung to all four corners of the room. But Fergal doesn't scold me for being late. He can tell by my face I've bad news.

"The Delaney boys have the fever," I say. "Murph and I have just been to see them. By the look of them, they're not long in this world."

"You pair finish up here." Fergal passes me the broom and runs his hand over the back of his head. "Rats we can catch. Food we can stretch. Sails we can stitch. But if fever be on board, I fear there isn't much we can do. I'll go tell the captain."

After he leaves, Mick and I sweep the mess into a pile and scoop it into a bucket.

"Seems a waste to throw it out." I say. "'Tis a whole bag of rice there."

Mick looks at me from under his brow. "Um ... Fergal said you're to pick out the rice ..."

"... grain by grain," I finish for him. I throw down the broom.

"Don't worry, Kit. I'll help you," he offers.

In silence, we sift through the mess, picking out the grains of rice and dropping them in a bowl. I wonder about the Delaneys, about the rest of us in the hold. I wonder about Coyle and what he remembers. I glance around the stacked barrels and wonder where Billy is now. I wonder if any of us are going to make it.

Mick winces and yanks his hand from the bucket. A tiny splinter of wood is rammed into his little finger.

"Coyle is awake," Mick says, fumbling with his finger. Try as he might, he can't grasp the sliver's end. "He's groggy, but Fergal figures he'll be good as new soon enough, though his hand is still broken."

I think about how angry Coyle will be. One-handed or not,

he's still a danger. "Captain says we've two weeks or so to go before we see land," I say, "maybe less if the other ship has the materials for the mast repair. Can you keep out of Coyle's way? Do you think you can do that?"

He considers the question and answers without looking up. "I'll avoid Coyle if you avoid Joe Murphy."

The cheek of him! "What's that supposed to mean? He's my friend. Are you telling me who I can and can't have as a friend now?"

Mick shrugs, ears blazing red, as he consumes himself with his damn sliver. I know he's avoiding the question.

"Oh, for God's sake, give it to me," I take his hand in mine but the sliver is in deep. Even I can't snag the start. I seem to be driving it in further. "Quit your fidgeting," I scold, but he keeps tugging every time I think I've got a piece of it. "Mick! Stop being such a baby. For once, take it like a man."

He yanks his hand away hard and I know my words have cut him deeply. I didn't mean anything by it. Not really.

"Do you want it infected? Is that it?" I rant, as though a sliver is the worst thing that has happened on this Godforsaken ship.

"You want to land in Canada after surviving this whole bloody journey, Coyle, the fever, the storms, the whole blessed lot of it—and fall over dead from an infected finger?" I'm exaggerating now. But I can't stop myself. I stand. "Well, go right ahead, Mick O'Toole. Be my bloody guest. 'Twill only prove to the world how bloody thick-headed you bloody well are. This sliver, the fever, Coyle, Smythe—sure, what does it matter? Jump over the railing for all I care! Go ahead and get yourself killed! Either way you end up dead and I—" My voice catches. "I am left alone."

My heart is pounding. Where did all that come from? And why was I dumping it on Mick?

Because he can take it. Because he's strong. Solid. Because in all the years I've known him, indeed our whole lives together, Mick has always been there. As familiar to me as my old hearthstone. Mick is my rock, no matter how my temper flares and my words burn.

He stands then. Holds his splintered hand out to me.

Without a word, I bring his finger to my lips, grasp the sliver with my teeth and draw it out. "There," I mumble. "Now, was that so hard?" I let go of his hand. But he holds on to mine.

"I won't leave you, Kit. Ever." He stares at the floor. "I … I love you."

He looks at me then, waits for my words, but they won't come out. They're jammed inside me. I feel them there, stinging just beneath the surface. A man might know to grasp them with his lips and draw them out of me, but Mick doesn't.

"Is it so hard to love me?" he asks, but it isn't a question. He lets go of my hand.

Oh, Mick.

My silence hurts him. He nods once and heads up the stairs. I should call after him. Should run to him and try to explain. But can't he see?

I can't love anyone else. Mam, Jack, Annie, Lizzie, Da— everyone I have loved I have lost.

And I can't lose him. Not Mick. For, as much as he drives me crazy, I realize 'tis Mick I need the most now.

CHAPTER FOURTEEN

I stand in the storeroom and watch Mick leave, but I can't bring myself to say anything.

"Boy, Kenny," Billy says, and I jump at the sound of his voice. In all the commotion, I'd forgotten he was in the storeroom with us as well. "You and your brother sure are close."

I see him in the shadows of the far corner, slipping a loose floorboard back in place before he comes to join me. I wondered where he hid when he wasn't in the barrel.

"He's not my brother," I say, still raw from the exchange with Mick. I hadn't meant to tell anyone the truth. Least of all, someone I barely know. Still, Billy trusted me with his secret.

Surely, I could trust him with mine.

"And my name is not Kenny, either." It feels good to speak the truth after weeks of living this lie. I lived it to protect myself. But so many times I wanted to tell everyone who I really was, to whisper it to Joe, to jump on the table and cry it out from my gut.

"I'm Kathleen Byrne," I finally say. It feels like I've let out a breath I'd been holding far too long. "Kit."

"A girl?" Billy's eyes widen in shock and then smile in awe. "Wait till the lads hear that Coyle got his bell rung by a girl!"

"No!" I blurt. "They can't know. No one can, Billy." I tell him my story then. Of how I tried to kill Lynch. Of the price on my head. Of Mick's idea to disguise me as his brother Kenny O'Toole. I feel like I am confessing to Father Doolen, except for the fact that my sins seem to impress Billy.

"Did he die, then?" Billy asks, eyes shining. "Is Lynch good and dead?"

"Either way, I'm a criminal. I tried to murder him, Billy. If I'm caught, I'm as good as dead." I shiver at the thought.

"A criminal," he whispers in awe, and rests his chin on his hands. "Tell me the part about the Lynch brothers again."

I don't really want to talk about it, don't want to relive it. I have spent weeks trying not to think about it. I even envy Coyle's memory loss. It would be so simple to forget everything; to wipe the slate clean. But it doesn't work that way. Besides, Billy has been all alone for weeks in a storeroom full of food; he's starving for a good yarn and I've nothing else to be doing while I pick rice from wreckage. So I tell him my story. I sift through my memories as I say them, the good and the bad, sorting the ones I want to keep close.

Hours later, the ship's bell sounds for all hands on deck.

"That's odd," Billy says. "There's no storm. The sea is calm. What's he calling for?"

"Ahoy, *Wandsworth*!"

"Ahoy there!" a voice calls from over the water.

"The other ship!" I jump to my feet, careful not to spill the bowl of rescued grains. "They must be sending over something to fix our yard." My heart lifts at the thought. "We'll be in Canada in no time, once it's repaired!"

"Go and see," Billy says. "And I want to hear every detail when you come back!"

I take the steps two at a time, eager to see what's what. Smythe stands at the railing, ordering two sailors to pull the gangway door open, while two others lower a rope ladder toward the sea. Not a hundred yards away rests the *Wandsworth*, a huge ship, much like the *Erin*. Their sailors must be rowing over in a lifeboat.

I stand by Fergal and crane my neck for a better look as our sailors mill about the entrance and lean over the rail.

"Looks like we're getting our yard fixed," Fergal says. The sailors pull up ropes tied to a long pole. They pass it hand over hand and lay it along the deck. It's hard to credit a simple pole can make all the difference. Thank God the other ship had one to spare.

"We'll be in Canada in a week's time, Kenny," Fergal adds. "And not a moment too soon. Dr. Douglas works at Grosse Isle, where we land in Quebec. He might even be able to help the Delaney lads if they can hold on."

After five long weeks at sea, another week seems like forever. But Fergal's prediction stokes hope in places I thought were only ash. I look to the west over the ship's prow, anticipation burning within me.

Mam, Annie, Jack, I'm coming. I'm coming!

"Welcome aboard, men," Captain MacDonald says as three sailors climb up through the gangway entrance. They salute him and shake hands with our sailors. One of them turns back to offer a hand to the last two men coming up the rope ladder. The crowd parts and time slows like cooling sap, distorting, magnifying, trapping every detail.

A dark, curled head appears at the ladder's top.

His hand reaches out.

The sailors help him on board.

It can't be, it just can't.

I rub my eyes in disbelief.

Wake up, Kit! Wake up! For this must be a nightmare. But try as I might, I can neither wake nor run. I am trapped. As helpless as a fly in sap. Stuck where I stand, watching Tom Lynch come aboard the *Erin*.

"Can I have a word, Captain MacDonald?" his older brother Henry asks, as he climbs up next. "We know the criminal we seek is somewhere on board."

CHAPTER FIFTEEN

I can't move. I stand there not twelve feet away from the Lynch brothers, my mouth hanging open like a cod's, as helpless as a fish on deck. I'm dead if I stay here. I know that. Tom hasn't seen me yet, but he will.

Did they come all this way for me?

The sacrifice hardly seems worth it. Would they do that for justice? No. But revenge, that's a different story. People would sacrifice everything for a moment's revenge. Wasn't that what got me in this mess in the first place?

Someone yanks my arm. It's Mick, pulling me away. "Hide!" he whispers, shoving me toward the steps.

I stop halfway down when the captain speaks. "O'Toole? Do you mean Mick?"

"That's him!" Henry yells. Footsteps thump across the deck to where Mick stands at the top of the stairs. I crouch back against the wall. "Where is she? Kathleen Byrne. I know she's here."

"We went over this at port, sir," Captain MacDonald interrupts. "There is no Kathleen Byrne aboard. You saw for yourself."

"You're from Killanamore, aren't you?" Henry continues, ignoring the captain. "Who's traveling with you?"

Mick doesn't answer.

"Who's traveling with him?" Henry repeats.

My heart thumps in my chest.

Mick doesn't answer.

"His younger brother," Coyle says for him. "Kenny."

"That's got to be her," Henry says. "You said she was wearing breeches, didn't you, Tom?"

"I might have," Tom says. "But I've told you a thousand times since, Henry. I'm not sure. Not really."

The sailors murmur amongst themselves. A few chuckle.

"Beat by a girl, eh, Coyle?" a voice calls.

"Glad to see she went easy on you," another chides.

Captain MacDonald orders the sailors to fetch Kenny O'Toole from the hold to settle all this business. I hear them walk to the far hatch and call for me. Legs trembling, I retreat inch by inch, praying the steps won't creak. Praying I can make it back to the storeroom.

"She's here! I've found her!" Coyle's voice yells from the top of the stairs. I try to escape down the last few steps but he lunges, knocking the wind out of me. We tumble forward and I bang my head against the steps and wall as we clatter to the bottom. I land face first, but before I can catch my breath, Coyle wrenches my arms to my back where he grips them in one hand. His other hand grips the scruff of my neck like I'm some mewling kitten. "You'll curse the day you ever set foot on this ship," he growls for my ears alone.

My secret's out. Not only am I a girl, I'm a wanted criminal!

The men argue amongst themselves about what to do with me as I stand before them on deck. They've tied my hands behind my back, shackled my feet, as though I've anywhere to run.

"She should be keelhauled," Smythe suggests. Coyle smiles

and agrees.

"She's paid for passage." Captain MacDonald corrects him.

"Give her to us," Henry Lynch demands. "We have a warrant. She is our quarry." His eyes glitter with an intensity that makes me shudder.

"She is neither stowaway," the Captain looks at Smythe and then Henry, "nor prey." As he turns his eyes to me, I cannot read his expression. All I know is that this is his ship, his jurisdiction. My fate rests in his hands alone. For now.

He takes a deep breath. "But she is a wanted criminal."

My shoulders sink with the weight of it.

Henry steps forward, eager to take me, but the captain holds up a hand. "She has paid for her passage to Canada. I'll not deny her that." He nods at Coyle. "Lock her up in the storeroom. When we reach Quebec, I'll give her over to the authorities. They can decide her fate."

The men clamor around the Captain, trying to persuade him otherwise, while Coyle leads me down to the storeroom. Already my ankles are rubbed raw by the rusty cuffs. Coyle shoves me against the thick post in the far corner of the room while he attaches my shackles to it. He yanks the chain to be sure there's no chance of escape.

"Don't worry about being handed over to Lynch in Quebec," he says, raising himself to his full height in front of me. He smiles, savoring the moment, before his meaty backhand strikes my face, knocking me to the ground. "You have to make it there, first."

CHAPTER SIXTEEN

The chains tether me to the post like some wild animal. Though I suppose that is what I am. Or, at least, how they're treating me. The captain did me no favors putting Coyle as my warden. At least Fergal comes with him to open the storeroom. At least I'm not alone with Coyle, for he'd surely beat me like an old rug.

With only a strand of light hemming the door to measure the passing of time, my eyes are used to the darkness. I'm worse than a rat now, preferring the shadows. The sound of Fergal's key jangling in the lock makes me squint, readying myself for the daylight that presses upon my eyes until they ache. Coyle follows behind, carrying my cup and bowl. Fortunately, the captain insisted that each paid passenger got their rations. Unfortunately, mine are delivered by Coyle. My throat is bone dry, itching for a taste of that water. Looking over his shoulder at Fergal who is rummaging among the barrels, Coyle sets everything just out of reach.

"Looks like you're going to make it to Quebec after all," Coyle sneers. "We'll make port within the week."

Fergal hefts a half empty bag of rice onto his shoulder. "And none too soon, by the look of it." He walks over to hand Coyle the bag. Noticing my cup and bowl are out of reach, Fergal squats and pushes them beside me. Turning to pick up another bag of rice, he misses seeing Coyle's yellowed spit drop like seagull poop, splashing in the center of my cup.

"Enjoy your supper," Coyle's face slides into his malicious grin.

He can do what he likes to my food. I'll not be eating or drinking anything served by his hand. Moments after the door shuts behind them and my eyes adjust to the darkness, I see him pop up from the shadows like a jack-in-the-box. Billy. God knows where I'd be without him.

"Would you not let me clout that eejit with another box, Kit?"

he whispers as he scrounges among the barrels and boxes for today's meal.

"I'd like nothing better, Billy. But another crate to the head might remind him of how he got that first clatter. We're lucky he hasn't remembered you're here."

Moments later, Billy hands me a cup of water that I down in one gulp. It does nothing to quench the fire in my throat. I wipe the sweat off my forehead.

"Dinner is served, m'lady," he says, passing me a bit of mushy apple and some dried out cheese from the Cunninghams' stores. "Alone, they're so rotten they're barely edible" he says, alternating bites between the cheese and apple. "But together, they're not bad." He spits out a pit. "We should be eating their good food, for the Cunninghams will probably have a great turkey dinner waiting for them when they arrive at Quebec."

"All I have waiting for me is a long trip home to Ireland." I think of Henry's glittering eyes. "Or a short trip to the afterlife." Though for weeks I've yearned to make port, now the thought of it terrifies me.

"Don't fret, Kit," he says, patting my leg, careful not to

touch my raw and oozing ankles. "There's a bit of hope in every calamity. Like that silver seam around the door, you just need a bit of it to find your way."

Famine, fever, families rent apart. There's no hope in any of that. Though I'm glad of his company, Billy doesn't know what he's talking about. He tries to keep my hopes up, but I may as well be chained to a sinking ship. Nothing could possibly save me now.

In the distance, the bell tolls. Another soul has died.

CHAPTER SEVENTEEN

One day rolls into the next, marked only by a thin seam of light around the door or the distant clang of the ship's bell, as though in a dream. With nothing to do but worry, I fear for those I love. For Mam and Jack. For little Annie. For Mick. I haven't seen him since my arrest. I drift from one nightmare into another.

"Here, Kit. Drink," Billy says, putting a cup in my hand.

Though my throat is on fire, I can barely lift my head, let alone my arm.

"Kit … are you all right?"

His voice floats from beyond as though I've fallen down the long, dark tunnel. I can barely hear him over the low drumming noise. Beating. Beating. Beating like a great bodhran as the darkness presses in.

Is this the fairy tomb? I'm buried alive!

Cold hands touch my face. "Jaysus, you're on fire!"

Though I can't open my eyes, my burning face tells me the flames are surely higher than our bonfires back home. Heat radiates from every part of me. Forging my joints together so that I cannot move. Melting my mouth so that I cannot speak. Leaving me helpless to do anything but lie against my post and burn.

Like a martyr.

No. Like a witch.

Something grips my shoulders and lowers me to the ground. Pours cold water on my face. I can almost hear the hiss and sputter.

The drumming hurts my head. I just want it to stop.

I just want it all to be over.

CHAPTER EIGHTEEN

The light blinds me. Sears through my eyelids and burns into the back of my head. I try to moan, but my throat is ash. I try to move, but my bones are welded tight.

Voices echo around me. Whispers fade in and out.

"... covered in rash ..."

"... fever ..."

"... is she alive?"

I must be dead. My lips won't part.

Sewn shut?

My lids, too heavy to open.

Held closed with two big brown pennies?

I am here, yet not. So, I'm not bound for heaven after all.

What did you expect? You tried to kill a man.

My body burns, my blood scalds my very veins, and yet I cannot cry out.

So this is hell.

Hands lift me and lay me on a sheet. Wrap me tight.

My shroud.

They carry me up the stairs into the light. It shines blood red through my heavy lids. The sea air I wanted for so long slaps my face as I am laid out on the deck. Nausea washes over me, but I haven't the energy left to get sick.

So this is it. This is how it ends.

I wait for the bell. The drop. The splash. I wait for the eternal sinking. For the frigid sea to snuff my burning body. But instead, the water spills over my mouth.

A shadow cuts the burning sun. Someone leans over me, cradling my head. "Drink, Kit. Please, love."

Da?

I try to drink for him but then everything goes black.

CHAPTER NINETEEN

"Can you not take her now, Father?"

Who ... Da?

God Almighty?

Someone's cool hands touch my side, feel my forehead.

"I'm sorry, son," the deep voice near me answers. The accent is foreign to me. Not Irish. Not Da. "Grosse Isle, she is already overflowing with patients."

"But she'll die here."

So I'm not dead. Not yet, anyway.

A thumb draws a cross on my forehead. "Through this holy anointing may the Lord in his love and mercy help you with the grace of the Holy Spirit ..."

The whisper of Latin prayers mingles with the scent of holy oil. The Last Rites. The sacrament for the dying.

A priest, then.

'Twould be so easy to let go. A part of me wants to. No pain. No sorrow. Nothing. I want to sleep forever. But something in me screams out.

I don't want to die!

He anoints my eyes, ears, nostrils, lips, hands, and feet. "Through this holy unction and His own most tender mercy may the Lord pardon thee whatever sins or faults thou hast committed."

Forgiveness?

No! Pray that I survive. *Pray that I find my family.*

The thought of them rushes through me like a bolt of lightning, grounding me in my body. I gasp. With all I have left in me, I will my eyes open. My head throbs and I moan.

"Kit!" Mick is at my side, stroking my hair. "You're awake. Praise the Lord, 'tis a miracle." He looks to the priest, but he has already turned to the people lying next to me on the deck.

"Lynch," I croak, lying there as vulnerable as a chick from its shell. Surely he'd be swooping in for me any second. I try to sit up but everything spins.

"Lie still. Tom has the fever and the captain has quarantined them to their room. You're safe for now."

I swallow, though it makes my throat burn. Mick puts a cup of water to my lips. "We made it, Kit," Mick says, tilting the cup. "Canada. We're here."

"Let me see," I mumble.

"Rest, now. You'll see—"

"Let me see!"

He wraps my rash-covered arm around his shoulder. The sight of it shocks me. I can only imagine how the rest of me looks. Mick carries me the few steps to the railing where he settles me on my feet. I have no strength. My legs shudder and buckle beneath me, but Mick holds me up. Every joint in my body aches. My head pounds. But I have to see. I can't believe him until I see it with my own eyes.

After weeks of nothing but unbroken horizons and the ship's darkness, my eyes feast on this rugged shore. I gorge myself on it from one end to the other. Up the rocky bluff on the far left, along weathered tree tops, and past the tall pole laden with colored flags. Passengers load on the steamer at the dock straight ahead. Behind the dock, a path winds through the small village of tents. Houses. A church. Green grass. On the right, a few more buildings, three cannons, and more rocky inlets. A flock of seagulls lands on the wet stones and they settle their wings. The island's only a mile or so across, if that. But 'tis beautiful. I can't take my eyes off it.

Land.

A few people mill around the water's edge, washing perhaps. Knowing Mam, that would be the first thing she'd want to do.

My heart rushes at the thought of seeing them again. I'm so close now. As soon as we get ashore, I know I'll find them. Mam, Jack, Annie. They have to be there. They just have to.

But the *Erin* sits motionless a half mile from the shore. We aren't disembarking. We aren't even moving. I glance at the water around the island and catch my breath. So many ships. Thirty, maybe forty more, as well as ours, anchored at bay.

"Why are we waiting ..." The words snag on my dry throat like coarse wool on a briar.

"We're in quarantine, Kit," Mick says. He points at the bright yellow flag atop our mainmast and nods at the other ships. "We all are."

I see them then. The yellow flags, fluttering above the silent ships. Even if every ship had only a hundred passengers, that would mean ... thousands. Thousands of Irish who traveled that Godforsaken journey, forty days or more, only to be left waiting, dying at the shore's edge.

My family. Where is my family?

I search the forest of masts for the *Dunbrody*. But there's no sign.

Are they on the island?

Did they make it?

I look back towards the ocean, not wanting to consider the thought that they were lost at sea. Worry blazes through my mind, burning away what little energy I have, and I close my eyes for a moment, trying to gather my strength. Gently, Mick lowers me to the deck.

"Father Robson," cries Mrs. Ryan; she's lying beside me. "Please, don't leave me!"

"The other passengers in the hold, they wait for me, too," he says, prying Mrs. Ryan's bony fist from his black sleeve before he stands. "Do not worry, Madame. Rest now. I am no doctor, but I say you have not the ship fever."

"And I'm no doctor, neither, Father. But I'd say with sick and sound together, 'twon't be long before we all have it."

Father Robson kneels again beside her; he seems so large beside her frail frame as he takes her hand and pats it.

"Wait for death, Father?" Mrs. Ryan asks. "Is that all I can do?"

He reaches in his cassock and, pulling out his black rosary beads, places them in Mrs. Ryan's twisted fingers. "You can pray.

Pray for me and I will pray for you. Dr. Douglas is coming soon. He's on the *Royalist* right now. After he inspects your ship, you will come to the island. And when you come to Grosse Isle, you can give me back my rosary beads."

He smiles at her and then at me as I lie back on the deck. I notice the dark circles under his eyes. He turns and walks to the hold steps. He's a big man, Father Robson. Solid. Strong. A farmer's son, perhaps.

I wonder how many tired souls he carries on those broad shoulders.

GROSSE ISLE

CHAPTER TWENTY

"Water! Water! Please, somebody!"

The crying wakes me.

"Help me. I need help!" The pleas come from beside me, beyond me, all around me. I realize then that I'm crying it, too. Joining in the sorrowful chorus.

"Water ... please ..." My throat burns like a hearth of embers.

A young priest raises my head and puts a cup to my lips. "Here."

My eyes try to focus on the white canvas roof above him.

Where am I? Where's Mick and Murph and Joe?

But none of it really matters as he tilts the tin cup. All I care about are those precious drops of water washing down my burning throat.

"Yes, Father McGauran?" a woman's voice says.

He gently lowers my head to the ground and turns to the woman. "Nurse, these patients have been in here for eighteen hours without any assistance!"

"More nurses have quit," she says. "We haven't enough staff."

"These poor people haven't even had a drink of water!" Father McGauran's voice rises with anger. Then he lowers it to a whisper. "Will we let them die for want of a cup of water?"

"They've assigned me to *three* tents *and* the hospital. The sick keep coming. I can't do it all. I just can't." She breaks into tears and covers her face with her hands. "I am only one person! What difference can one person make?"

I roll onto my side in the smothering heat, finding some relief in the damp ground beneath me. The scant bits of straw laid down for bedding fail to cover the mud. My elbow sinks slightly as I lean on it to hand the tin cup to the woman calling for a drink beside me. She takes it in her hands and, trembling, brings it to her dry lips.

Father McGauran points at me. "Look there. I helped her and she helps others. One person can make a difference. You do make a difference."

"But, Father," she answers, her voice empty of all hope as they walk away. "What good are two, or even four, when there are thousands?"

My arm shakes as I push myself up further to sit. I'm in a tent of sorts, about fifty feet long, every inch of its floor covered with sick people, a hundred of them or more squeezed in side by side. A living, breathing mass of men, women, and children, all crying out for water. Bony arms reach up here and there for help as Father McGauran and the nurse pick their path through the bodies, stooping to give a drink now and then.

I have to find my family. If they are here in this tent recovering, they need me more than ever. I push myself up and try to stand, but my legs buckle like a newborn lamb's. My head feels fuzzy, thick with wool. But I can't just sit here. Not when my family is so close. With all my strength, I stand. After some moments of swaying, I take a few faltering paces. Despite my best attempts to avoid it, I step on a few people. Some cry out. Others don't even notice. The ground seems to tilt from side to side like a ship in a squall, and I stagger, before tumbling into the arms of a man entering the tent.

"Easy there." He catches me and lowers me to the ground by the door, sitting me in a tiny space between two other patients. Kneeling before me, he touches my forehead and the sides of my throat. "How are you feeling?"

"Shaky," I say. "It feels like I'm still on the boat."

He smiles. "'Twill take you a few hours to get your land legs. After a while, the ground will feel solid again. Even I catch myself still listing to one side."

"Were you on a ship?" I ask, for he has an Irish accent. From Kilkenny, I'd say. "I thought you were a doctor."

"The *Wandsworth*," he nods and checks inside my mouth. "We just arrived. But I am a doctor. Name's Benson. As much as I'd like to continue my journey inland, I can't very well leave you all like this, now, can I?"

"I'm looking for my family," I say. "The Byrnes on the *Dunbrody*. Do you know where they are?"

He shakes his head.

"Well, what about Mick O'Toole or the Murphys then, from the *Erin*, my ship?" I don't bother naming Billy. If he survived, he'll not be registered anywhere.

"They might be in here. This tent is mainly those from the ships debarked in the last two days, and they do try to keep families and shipmates together." His eyes soften as he lays me back down. "Rest now. Your fever has broken but the rash will take a few days to clear. I'll send in some broth for you. Do you think you can eat?"

He smiles at my nod. "That's a good sign. Give yourself a chance to recover, a day or two, and then you can ask at the records office about your family. They log every ship."

He opens the flap and calls for an orderly to bring me in a bowl of broth. I thank Dr. Benson for his help and watch him wade deeper into the sea of bodies. The orderly enters and hands me a steaming bowl. It warms me, revives me at the core. I drain every last drop before heading for the door.

Rested or not, I have to find my family.

CHAPTER TWENTY-ONE

"Kit!" A voice calls as I near the tent door.

"Murph!" I weave through the maze of patients to the man lying in the far corner. He grabs my hand and pulls me down for a hug. We are surrounded by strangers, though I recognize Mrs. Ryan next to him, eyes closed, rosary beads gripped in her knotted hands.

"I thought we'd lost you," he says, his voice hoarse. "People were saying you'd be at the Lynches' mercy once we laid anchor."

I notice the nurse and Father McGauran are away at the other end of the tent. "Do you want a drink of water?"

Murph nods and I fetch him one. Just going to the water

barrel by the pole at the center of the tent exhausts me. But it gives me a chance to check the patients. There is no sign of my family in those rows of sorry souls. I give him the cup and then rest my trembling hand against his burning forehead. Opening his shirt, I press on his rashy chest but the white handprint I so want to see doesn't appear. He's worse than I thought.

"Where's everyone else?" I say. "Mick, Joe, and Brigid?" I'm almost afraid to ask.

"The sailors and soldiers took the healthy off the ship. I think they're keeping them on another end of the island. Billy, he's with them, too." He coughs and finishes his water. "You're full of secrets, aren't you, Kit?" he says with a weak smile.

"I'm sorry I lied to you, Murph, about who I am."

He squeezes my hand. "Kit or Kenny, 'tis all the same. I know who you are."

"Rest now," I say. "I'm going to check this tent for our families."

But he won't let go of my hand. Instead, he lowers his voice. "Keep clear of those Lynch lads, Kit. By the look of Henry Lynch, he'll do what he likes whether he has the law on his side or not."

He stops to catch his breath and glance around at the sleeping bodies by us. "Watch yourself."

He closes his eyes for a moment. The talking has worn him out. "If you see them, my Joe and wee Brigid ... if you see them before I do, Kit, would you tell them they've got all they need. Sure, haven't they the Murphy spirit? Tell them that."

I promise him I will. Though I doubt I'll see them in here if they're not sick. From what Dr. Benson said, Tom and Henry Lynch could be in this tent. I look over my shoulder where the sick, the dying, and the dead lie in long, rank rows. Most suffer from dysentery as well as fever and are too weak to do anything but wallow in their filth. If the Lynches are here, they're in no shape to pursue me. Still, I have to be careful.

I drag myself to my feet and wander up and down the rows of people. There must be over a hundred. Some ask for water or about their own missing families; most just lie in the grip of the fever, moaning and unconscious.

"Water ... please ..." A hand grabs my leg. "Kit?"

It's Tom Lynch. Without even thinking, I jerk my foot away and get ready to bolt. But a second look at the state of him tells me he's no threat. He'd no strength in his grip; sure, he can barely raise his head. His face is flushed with fever; it covers his body, as though he'd rolled in a nettle patch. The people all around him are strangers, most unconscious.

"Water, Kit ... please ... I ..."

A part of me wants to stand there and watch him burn for what he did to my house. My family. He threw that torch onto our roof. He burned my home right before my eyes. The Lynches kept me off the *Dunbrody*, separated me from Mam, Jack, and Annie.

"Where is Henry?" I ask, looking around. The stranger lying next to Tom is dead. His vacant eyes stare up after his spirit. From the look of Tom, he's not far off himself, but Henry Lynch is nowhere to be seen.

"Gone." Tom closes his eyes and swallows. He grimaces from the pain. "He didn't want to catch it."

It doesn't surprise me to hear that Henry would abandon his own. Kneeling, I raise Tom's head in my hand and hold the cup to his chapped lips, for he hasn't even the strength to take it himself. Most of it spills down his chin. He coughs and I lay his head back. His hair is sopping wet, the black curls stick to his forehead.

"I had to find you ..." he says, gripping my hand like a drowning man.

"I'm not going back to jail. You can't—"

"No, Kit," his eyes strain to hold on mine. "I wanted to see you, to tell you ... I'm sorry ... for everything."

Sorry, says he. Like that makes any difference to me. Empty words, now.

"The day you left Ireland aboard the *Erin*," he continues, "I told Henry I saw you. I thought he'd give up the hunt once he knew you'd left the country." His breath is shallow. All this talk is burning up what little energy he has left. "But Henry wants—"

"Revenge," I finish for him.

He shakes his head. "Da put a reward on your head. A big one. Used our inheritance money." He pauses to catch his breath. "Henry won't stop until that money is his."

So that was why Henry came after me. He's to bring me back to Ireland if he wants his inheritance. Lynch must have known what sort of animal he was unleashing on me, for Henry's greed is worse than his temper. He won't rest until I'm behind bars again. Not if my freedom costs him his inheritance.

"You came all this way to tell me that? To warn me?" I ask, remembering the dreadful journey.

"No." He grips my hand in both of his. "I came for you, Kit. I haven't stopped thinking of you. I had to tell you I'm sorry and … and … that I care about you."

I can't speak. I'd waited so long to hear him say those words, but not like this. Not here. Not now.

"Tom, I—"

"I know what you did. I forgive you. I do."

I pull my hand away. "But I'm not sorry, Tom." Only sorry I didn't kill his father and his brother, too, come to think of it.

I look away.

What sort of monster have I become?

"Kit, forget about the past."

I don't think Tom has much of a future. Days, maybe, if that.

"If you can't give me your love," he pleads, "will you give me your forgiveness, then?"

Maybe if I'd found my family I could. Maybe if I knew they were alive and well.

I look at the boy of my dreams lying in the mud, begging

with his eyes. But I've neither love nor forgiveness for him, and I cannot give what I haven't got.

"A cup of water, Tom. 'Tis all I have to give you."

And leaving the tin cup in his trembling hand, I turn and walk away.

CHAPTER TWENTY-TWO

I hand out cup after cup of water, asking anyone that's awake for information, but no one knows anything about the *Dunbrody*. Hours later, I kneel between Murph and Mrs. Ryan; I can hardly hold myself up.

"They're not in this tent but my family *is* on this island, Murph. I feel it. They must be in one of the other tents." I look at the door a few feet away. It seems like miles. "I'm going to look for them."

Murph takes my hand. "Will you stay here with me, Kit?"

I want to leave, to start my search. I don't want to waste another moment. But I've barely the energy take one more step.

Besides, Murph needs me. I lie beside him.

"We made it, Murph. To Canada, just like you said. Thank God, that great journey is over."

"The great journey is over," he repeats, a smile warming his words. "And so begins another." He weakly squeezes my hand.

I open my eyes, relieved to have a clear head. My body, though stiff from sleeping on the damp ground, is free from the fever's shiver and ache. I turn to see how Murph is, but he's gone. So is Mrs. Ryan. In fact, the whole place seems much less crowded, though the orderlies and a few sailors are carrying in new patients and laying them in the empty spaces. Father Robson's rosary beads lay in the dirty straw where Mrs. Ryan had been. I pick them up and put them in my pocket for safekeeping. After a half-hour, Murph still hasn't returned.

A young sailor carries in a woman and lays her next to me.

"Oh, that's my friend's place," I say, but the sailor makes no motion to move the woman elsewhere. Instead he turns to leave.

"She can't stay there." I stand and follow him to the door as he pulls the tent flap open. A village of tents sprawls before us.

Near two hundred of them. I grab his thick arm, stopping him. "Are they ..." my mind staggers at the sheer numbers, "... are they full of sick passengers, too?"

He nods. "Aye. So are those sheds." He points at a few long buildings. "They're stacked in bunk beds in there." He clenches his mouth. "You're better off here, and not like the wretched souls in the bottom bunks." He shakes his head in disgust. "The sheds, the tents, the hospital, even the chapel is crammed with sick. We've dozens of ships to unload and more arriving every day."

We stand for moment, speechless, as the reality of it all washes over us. So many sick. So many dying. And we are as powerless as two children trying to stop the tide.

I can't save them all, but I'll be damned if I don't save my own. "He's coming back," I say. "You'll have to move that woman. My friend, Murph, will be back soon."

The young sailor looks at me. "They don't come back here. There's only two places your friend could have gone." He points to the right, beyond the village of tents, across the bay to the east end of the island. "If your friend got better, then he's over there at the healthy side."

Murph wasn't well enough for that. Not yet.

"Otherwise," he nods to the left.

I step out of the tent and follow his gaze up the muddy field, past the log fence. In the distance, beside the mounds of dirt, two men lean on their shovels while four others toss up clods of earth from inside a trench. A wagon emerges from the road through the bushes to meet them, its bed piled high with newly made and newly filled coffins.

I close my eyes and turn to the east.

He's there. Healthy. Reunited with Joe and Brigid. He has to be. I won't believe anything else.

The sailor starts down the gravel path towards the wharf.

"The *Dunbrody*!" I call. If anyone knows about ships, it's him. "Have you seen her? Has she arrived?"

"Yes," he answers and my breath catches in my throat. "She arrived over two weeks back. I think some of her passengers are still in that tent up the hill."

Bolting from my tent, I stagger along the path, past tent after tent to the farthest one. The journey nearly kills me. My heart and head are throbbing as I bursting through the entrance.

"Mam!" I cry out, chest heaving. "Mam, where are you?"

An arm raises in reply, then another and another as every mother answers. My soul aches at the sight of so many families torn apart. In pleading voices, they call their children's names. But no one calls mine.

I pick my way through the sickly bodies, scanning gaunt faces, searching for Annie's curls, calling Jack's name. "Jack! Jack Byrne!"

"Stop that!" The lone nurse grabs my arm. "Quiet yourself. You're disturbing the patients."

"Jack!" I cry, pushing past her. "It's me! It's Kit! Are you in here?"

"I'm calling the soldiers," she warns as she exits.

"Who are you looking for?" a woman asks. She's rocking a child.

"My family. They were on the *Dunbrody*."

"I sailed on that ship," she says. "What was the family name again?"

"Byrne. Moira Byrne is my mother. Jack's twelve and my sister Annie is five. From Killanamore."

"Ronnie, do you know any Byrnes?" the woman calls over to a man up the way.

"Byrne?" he says, rubbing his chin and looking upwards. "From near Wicklow?"

"Yes! Yes! That's us!" I can hardly breathe. "Have you seen them?"

"There's a lad two rows over. I think he's a Byrne, if memory serves me right."

"Jack!" I cry, scrambling over the ragged piles and gaunt limbs. I have to see. I have to know.

And there he is. Jack. My Jack.

He's like a small scarecrow in his tattered clothes, nothing but skin and bone. A splattering of rash travels his arms and neck. Dark circles cup his eyes as he leans on another boy to stand.

"Kit?" he says and reaches for me.

"Jack … I found you!" I cry as I run to him and wrap my arms around him. We stand holding each other for ages. I don't want to let him go. Ever. Even Jack is clinging to me. "'Tis all right. I'm here now. Kit's here."

"You look like a boy," he finally says, wiping his eyes and

stepping back. He grins. "And a watery slip of a one at that."

Seeing him, being with him, makes me feel almost whole again.

"Oh, Kit," he says, "when we left New Ross without you, we thought the Lynches got you. We thought ..."

The soldier appears with the nurse and, seeing the joy of two ragged boys reuniting, chastises her for dragging him all this way for nothing. She scowls at us and goes back to her work.

I look behind Jack and around at the faces nearby. I don't recognize any of them. "Where's Annie?"

"She left on a steamer ship a few days ago."

"What? A steamer? Where? Why would Mam take Annie and leave you?"

"Annie's not with Mam, Kit," Jack explains. He speaks slowly. "They took the healthy children away. To orphanages."

"An orphanage?" I pause. "But Annie's not an orphan." As the words leave my lips, I see the sorrow on Jack's face.

"We're orphans, Kit."

Orphans.

The word sounds so terrible, its meaning too heavy to hold

on our tired shoulders.

"No, Jack. Don't. Don't say it." As if saying it makes it real.

"I'm sorry, Kit," he says, resting his hand on my shoulder. "Mam's gone. She died four days ago."

CHAPTER TWENTY-THREE

It hurts to think of her. To think she's gone. Instead, I throw myself into caring for Jack. Doing what Mam would have done for him were she here. I don't leave his side. He's weak, still battling the fever, but at least he is no longer alone. His friend Connor is a nice lad, a grand help, but I'm here now. I'll take care of Jack.

The rash goes white when I press on it, so it isn't a bad case. Not if it's cared for early. Sure enough, a day later, the fever breaks; he's taking soups and growing stronger. I have no more symptoms, thank God. In another few days, we'll be well enough to leave this cursed place and go find Annie. We will be together again. All of us. Just like Mam would have wanted.

"You're looking better, Kit," Father McGauran says. I wish I could say the same for him. He hasn't the fever, but he looks like he hasn't slept in days.

He leans over and feels Jack's forehead. "How is he?"

I've been picking the lice from Jack's clothes and hair while he slept. Lizzie always said fevers often followed them. I don't know if it makes any difference or not, but picking the nasty buggers makes me feel like I am doing something, and it stops some of his itching.

"Where is Dr. Benson?" I ask. He usually does the rounds in this tent while Father McGauran hears confessions and gives last rites.

Father McGauran clears his throat and wipes his sweaty forehead. "Sadly, he has caught the fever. A serious case. He is in one of the hospitals."

It hadn't occurred to me the danger in which these men and women put themselves to save us. Irish or Canadian, priests or pauper, soldiers or sailors, ditch diggers or doctors—the disease played no favorites. Any one of us could die from it.

"Will he recover?" I ask.

"I have given him his last rites. We've done what we can. It's in God's hands now." But the look in his eyes makes me think Dr. Benson hasn't long in this world.

"He should have left on the steamer," I say, thinking of his decision to stay. "He wasn't sick from the journey."

"But by staying, Dr. Benson saved many lives," Father McGauran says, "even if it cost him his own."

I don't argue with him. Sure, isn't he himself doing the very same thing? Bishop's orders or not, I'd be on the first steamer out of here if it was me. Miles away, just like many of the workers eager to be off this death island. 'Tis supposed to be an entry into Canada, not an exit to the afterlife.

Father McGauran kneels down beside me. "You've recovered. Tomorrow you will be sent upriver on the steamers."

"But I can't—" I blurt. There is no way I'm leaving Jack. Ever.

Father McGauran holds up his hand. "Perhaps we can help each other. Many nurses have quit and Dr. Douglas, the Superintendent here at Grosse Isle, said to hire who we can. But the priests and I can find no one willing to stay and work."

It doesn't surprise me.

"You can stay in this tent and be close to your brother," he adds. "And I can pay you. It isn't much, but it is something."

I need money. I hadn't thought of that.

"I will," I finally say. "But only until Jack is well."

Father McGauran smiles and shakes my hand. He holds it then and pauses. "Since I'm here, would you like to make a confession?"

I suppose my face is filthy with guilt. Bad enough I tried to kill a man. Worse yet, I've no shame nor sorrow about it. No doubt, the sin emanates from me like fever rot. But the hammering of coffins, the sight of so many in sorrow and grief, the stink of sickness and death, it overwhelms me. I can't confess my sins when I wish I'd poisoned every rotten-hearted landlord that caused this cursed event.

What sort of a landlord lets this happen to his people?

What sort of a God does?

I blush and look away from Father McGauran, afraid he'll see my dark thoughts.

"No, no thank you, Father," I whisper, careful not to wake Jack. "The sick need you more."

"Sickness comes in many forms," he says, though I know the truth of it. He pats my hand. "Hold on to your faith, Kit. God is greatest in our weakness."

But his words don't matter. We are getting stronger, Jack and I. I'm going to save my family and I don't need anybody's help.

Not even God's.

CHAPTER TWENTY-FOUR

Over the next few days, I tend to the people in Jack's tent. My clothes are soaked with sweat as I carry food and water to the patients. Father McGauran tells me it's only mid-June, yet. Surely, it can't get any hotter. 'Tis already a living hell.

I've given Jack the last of my herbs from Lizzie. But for the other poor souls I can only give cool cloths for their hot faces and cups of cold barley water or lemonade. Be it their fever or the cursed heat that smothers us all, they can't get enough to drink. Some get hot gruel and meat, if they have an appetite. But many are hungry for nothing. They stare listlessly at the canvas roof, starved of everything, even the will to live.

There is no news from the east end of the island. Father McGauran tells me they, too, are in quarantine, for the fever didn't always show signs at first. If they are well enough after the ten days, they head up the Saint Lawrence to towns on the mainland. It's been over a week since the *Erin* arrived, since I saw my friends. I wonder about Billy, Brigid, and Joe. But most often, my thoughts turn to Mick.

Where is he? How is he? Will I ever see him again?

"The passengers from the *Imogene* will be placed here," Father McGauran says, nodding at the far corner. "It will be a tight fit, but we are out of tents and sheds, and the chapels are full of patients, too."

I hand him a cup of lemonade. He smiles, but it doesn't reach his eyes.

I'd heard the *Imogene* sank off the coast of Cape Breton. I can only imagine the terror those poor people must have lived through until the *Niger* arrived to rescue them. The tragic stories just never seem to end. I wipe my hand across my forehead, pushing the sweaty hair off my face.

"Why don't you take a break, Kit? Get some air. You'll make

yourself sick again. You don't want Jack sent off without you," he adds.

He's right. Jack is sleeping. His color is good and he just ate a full meal. I, on the other hand, feel like death warmed over.

I nod and leave the tent, but the air is just as hot and heavy outside. Thinking I should find out about Annie's steamer, I walk the dirt path around the bay towards the records office. Another thirty or more new ships are anchored in the Saint Lawrence, waiting for their inspection. Yellow flags flutter atop long masts, like sick leaves on rotting stalks.

At the edge of the bay, Dr. Douglas climbs into a rowboat beside Father Robson. A sailor shoves out from the shore and begins hauling on the oars. Day after day. Ship after ship. The two men row back and forth between the island and the boats. Just behind them, at the far left side of the bay, the three cannons point out to the water. They're there to ensure boats stop for inspection but, just yesterday, I'd heard a captain say that it would be more merciful to sink the ships than to let the passengers suffer such a slow death. The *Erin* was lucky. Many ships wait for days, sometimes weeks, in quarantine.

Father Robson glances back to where I stand by the shore.
Remembering his rosary in my pocket, the one left behind by
Mrs. Ryan, I pull it out and hold the black beads over my head.
Surely he'd want it back. I wave and point at his rosary dangling
from my other fist. He raises one hand and nods.

He thinks I'm praying for him now.

I almost laugh at the thought, and me with my prayers as
empty as a rain barrel in a drought. But I put it back in my pocket.
I suppose the least I can do is hold on to it for him.

"Did you say Barnes?" the clerk asks, in the tiny office. I'd waited
ages in line for my turn.

"No, Byrne. Annie Byrne."

He squints at the log book as he runs his finger down the page.
"Boland … Brennan … Byrne. I've a Moira Byrne. Deceased
June seventh."

My throat tightens. "Yes, that's my mother. Is there nothing
about my sister, Annie? She left June eighth or ninth on a steamer.
I need to know where."

"Oh, an orphan?" He flips a few pages and repositions his

small round glasses. It feels like forever. "Father Cazeau has been working miracles finding homes for all these orphans." He flips through page after page. Name after name. There must be hundreds.

"Here," he says; his finger stops and so does my heart. "Annie Byrne, age five."

"Yes, yes, that's her!" I cry.

"Deported aboard the *Speed*." He trails his finger along the ledger. "For Bytown, June ninth."

I could jump across the counter and kiss him. "When does the next steamer for Bytown leave?"

He glances at a paper pinned to the wall beside him. "June eighteenth at ten o'clock."

Two days!

I turn to go, my heart soaring with the news.

"You're the second person to come looking for Annie Byrne," the clerk adds. It strikes me as odd. Surely Jack hasn't been down here. "Yes, now, what was his name? A big man with red hair ..."

"Lynch?" I say. A tingle runs down my spine. It can't be him.

He snaps his fingers. "That's the one. Henry Lynch. Said he was looking for her and her sister Kathleen."

So he hasn't given up. Not by a long shot. I feel sick.

The clerk glances at his book. "There's no record of Kathleen Byrne here. I told him he might find her in Bytown with Annie. Being sisters and all."

He looks at me over his glasses, standing there in my ragged pants and shirt with my dirty hair short and shaggy about my ears. "Funny, he never mentioned a brother."

CHAPTER TWENTY-FIVE

The crowd mills around at the wharf as the steamer approaches. We're all eager to be off this island. Although the doctors gave Jack a clean bill of health, he isn't fully healed. Truth be told, many of the people sitting along the wharf aren't. But I'd say their chances might be better off this island. Surely there are doctors and hospitals in Bytown.

Jack and Connor stand off to the side in deep conversation, no doubt saying farewell. Connor's family is making ready to board tomorrow's steamer bound for farther up the Ottawa River where many of their relatives have settled. I'd often heard Connor talking about their farms and lumber shanties.

Jack glances at me, long-faced. I know he's upset about leaving. But he needn't worry. He'll make new friends in Bytown.

I've said enough goodbyes to last me a lifetime, though I do have one more for Father McGauran, and I approach him as he steps onto the wharf. He thanks me for my help and wishes me well before handing me my wages. I put them in my pocket where they jangle against the rosary.

"Oh," I take out the black beads. "Can you give this to Father Robson for me?"

"He's caught the fever, been fighting the symptoms for some time now." He shakes his head. "Dr. Douglas is sending him to a hospital in Quebec. I fear he may not make it." He closes his hands around my fist of rosary beads. "Use it to pray for him. For all of us."

I've neither the heart to pray nor the words to tell him. Taking my silence as a yes, he squeezes my hands and then walks away.

"I'm going with Connor," says Jack, appearing beside me.

I've no idea what he's on about. Surely he's joking.

"His Da, Mr. Carey, will take me on as a hired hand," he continues, his voice picking up speed. "Mr. Carey says I can work the fields, and in the winter maybe I can help with the logging." He seems excited by the idea, like it might actually happen.

"Enough of your silliness, Jack." I nod at the steamer pulling up to the left side of the wharf and hold out his ticket. "Here, take this. 'Tis time to go."

"I'm not going with you, Kit," Jack says. He steps back and stands beside Connor. I look at the pair of them, barely out of short pants. Children, really.

"So you're just going to go off gallivanting with your pal, is that the way of it?" I ask. "What about Annie? What about your family?"

"I am thinking about my family. Sure, I'll be making real wages." His eyes light up. "I can send you some, just like Da would."

I laugh at him. He's only wee. "What do you know about taking care of the family?"

His lips tighten. I've hurt him, so I have. But he can't be serious.

What would Mam say? How did she get Jack to obey?

Worry squirms in my gut like a handful of cold worms. I know Jack. The more he's pushed the harder he pushes back. But

I have to be firm. Mam would. "Now, say goodbye to Connor and get on that boat."

Jack folds his arms and makes no move to follow me. People are boarding, handing their tickets to the captain. Panic wriggles inside me.

"I traveled to hell and back to find you. I nursed you back to health. You almost died, Jack. You would have if it weren't for me!" I'm yelling now. People are staring.

Let them stare. I've had enough of this nonsense.

I point my finger at Jack. "I didn't save you so you can go off and kill yourself on some foolish adventure. You *are* going to Bytown! We *are* going to find Annie! I *will* bring this family together, God help me!" I point at the boat, hand on my hip. "Now get on that bloody steamer!"

"You are not Mam!" Jack snaps. The words sting like the tail of a whip. "Stop trying to tell me what to do!" Anger flushes his face and his fists are balled at his side. "Where were you when Mam was sick on the boat? When Annie cried? When Mam took her last breath?" His mouth trembles with the memory of it. "Who do you think took care of the family then, Kit? Not you.

'Twas me! Me! I did!"

"And look what a great job *you* did," I spit bitterly. The words rush out of me like vomit, hot and horrible. I can do nothing but heave them upon him. "Annie's gone. Mam is dead. 'Tis a good thing I got here when I did or I'd have no brother left, either."

Jack glares at me, jaw clenched. In all our years of bickering, I'd never seen such hatred in his eyes.

"Too late," he answers through gritted teeth. "For you've no brother anymore."

And just like that, he turns and walks away.

CHAPTER TWENTY-SIX

The captain calls out and the passengers board. I barely hear them over the thumping of my heart as I watch Jack walk away with Connor.

He can't mean it. He'll turn around any second now.

Only he doesn't. He just keeps walking up the hill.

"Jack!" I shout. "If we don't find Annie soon, we may never find her at all. She's already a week ahead of us." But he doesn't turn around.

Curse you, Jack!

Had I the strength, I'd run after him and drag him on the bloody boat.

The selfish brat! How dare he walk away from me? Why must he be so bloody headstrong? I'm right. I know best. Why can't he see that?

"Are you boarding, lad?" the captain's voice calls.

I look at the boat. *I have to find Annie. I have to get to her before Henry Lynch does.* I look back up the hill. *But I can't leave Jack.*

"Kit?!" the name cuts through my fog as someone grabs my arm. "Sweet Jaysus, you're alive! You're alive!"

I'm smothered in an embrace.

"Mick?" I mumble into his ragged shirt. It feels good to see him, to be held, to let go and lean on someone else, if even for a moment.

He pulls me back and holds me at arm's length. "They wouldn't let me see you. The soldiers. I was nearly mad with not knowing how you were. I even tried sneaking over to the west side, but I kept getting caught. The last time I got this." He points at his fat lip and then hugs me again. "And here you are. My Kit. Alive and well."

His fat lip shines, taut in his grin, but the smile slides off his face when he sees my serious expression.

I tell him then about Mam and Annie and finally about Jack.

"Well, I'm bound for Bytown, too," he says and I realize he's jumped ship to get to me. "We just boarded the steamer on the east end of the island. I'll help you find Annie. We'll go to Bytown together, Kit." He smiles.

It comes to me then, a way to save both Annie and Jack. But Mick won't listen. Not if he thinks there's a future for us together in Bytown.

"Mick?" I ask, stopping him as he heads for the steamer. "Will you do something for me?"

"Anything, Kit. Just say the word."

I look up at him, knowing I'm asking for more than I deserve. "Will you … will you watch over Jack for me?"

His face drops.

"I need to know he's safe," I plead. "You're his friend, he'll listen to you. If anyone can convince him to come to Bytown, it's you, Mick."

Mick frowns. "Kit, no one can convince your brother of

anything he hasn't a mind to do himself."

"Please, Mick," I say, choosing my words carefully. "He's my family. Jack and Annie. They're all I've got."

I know I've hurt him. But I can't tell him I need him, for I know Jack needs him more. I can't tell him how I really feel about him or he won't stay with Jack.

He looks back at the steamer and up the hill at Jack walking away. A long breath escapes him as he settles his mind.

"All right, Kit," he finally says. "For you, I will."

I throw my arms around him. I don't want to let go. In all the places I have been these last long weeks, here in Mick's arms is the closest thing to home. He bows his head into my hair.

The steam whistle blows. It's time to go.

"Thank you, Mick," I say, though I know they aren't the words he wants to hear from me. I pull myself away and step onto the boat, pushing my way through the crowd to find the railing. To see Mick one last time.

He stands on the wharf, hands in his pockets. I think he is crying, or maybe the sun is just in his eyes.

How could I ask that of him? How could he say yes?

And yet we did.

I could wring Jack's neck for putting us all through this. If he'd only listened to me, we could all be going to Bytown together. The steamer draws back from the rocky shore and chugs westward, passing the tent-covered fields, the rocky bluff, the cemetery with its mass graves in long, mounded rows like large potato drills.

Goodbye, Mam.

I never did visit her grave. But what does it matter; she's not there. Not really. She's with Da now.

Mam always said their souls wove together like the spirals in a Celtic knot. She'd embroidered one on our kitchen curtain one summer when Da was away working in England. 'Twas a work of art, an intricate braid weaving over and under itself all along the border of the curtain, ending at a small bird's body in each corner. I hadn't realized the colorful braids were formed by the birds' long intertwining necks, so linked I couldn't tell where one started and the other finished.

"Love is like that, Kit," she'd said, running her finger over the detailed stitching.

"Confusing?" I'd asked and she'd laughed.

"Sometimes," she'd admitted. "But look at them. See how they reflect each other and support each other. They're one and the same, bound together even if they are miles apart."

I look back past the wake to the shrinking wharf. Mick stands where I left him on it, still staring after the boat. We've been through so much this past year, Mick and I. Lost so much. Survived so much. I don't know what I would have done without him. Our paths have always intertwined and I just can't picture mine without his. I slowly raise my hand and Mick does the same.

But I can't help wondering if I will ever see him again.

"Kit!" Billy, Joe, and Brigid push through the crowd and clamor around me; they're talking a mile a minute. Mick hadn't told me they were on the steamer. He hadn't told me all he was sacrificing.

"Did you know Henry was looking for you in the healthy sheds? Why are you going to Bytown?" They pepper me with questions.

Brigid yanks on my sleeve. "Did you see Grandad?"

I look at Joe; our eyes say it all. He didn't know. Not for sure. Squatting before Brigid, I hold her hand. "I did see him, pet. And he said to give you a message. One for you and Joe." I glance up at Joe. "He said to tell you you've got all you need right in here." I poke her chest. "Sure, haven't you the—"

"Murphy spirit," she finishes proudly. She slips her other hand in Joe's. "See, Joe? I told you. I wasn't just dreaming. 'Twas Grandad. He told me that before the angels came to take him to heaven."

Her faith moves me. I wish I could believe so wholeheartedly again.

"Your brother ... I mean, Mick," Joe says, "he's all right. I got to know him a bit better the last week together in the sheds."

"He near got himself killed a few times trying to find you, though," Billy continued. "The soldiers caught him twice sneaking through the bush and once trying to swim around by the shoreline."

I'd seen Mick's attempts at swimming back home. He'd tried it just the once and, God love him, he'd scrabbled and spluttered like a drowning cat.

"He never did stop trying to find you," Joe adds.

I wonder what lengths Mick would have to travel to find me now.

I wonder if he will.

BYTOWN

CHAPTER TWENTY-SEVEN

The steamer chugs along the river, spewing black smoke from its twin stacks as its wheel turns. Just being on a boat again makes me feel ill. I swore I'd never do it, but I have to find Annie. She is out there, somewhere. At least this time I'm not in the hold. At least now I've land in sight.

Brigid lies curled at my feet like a cat by the hearth as I stand with Joe at the ship's railing. I close my eyes and breathe deep for the first time in a long time, the fresh air such a blessing after my weeks in the stifling tents and clammy hold. Thick woods rise and fall along the rolling shoreline, broken here and there by a church spire or barn roof. Smoke trails from cottage chimneys, wispy reminders of normal lives. Lives I wonder if we'll ever live again.

The sicker passengers, those still feverish and rashy, lie in the large room beneath us. They're in worse condition than I thought. Far too ill to be discharged, let alone travel. Why separate us on the island only to throw sick and sound together on the steamer? But I suppose Dr. Douglas and his team can't handle so many. Even more yellow-flagged ships sat waiting in the bay as our steamer left. I only hope the people of Bytown are ready for us. We've been on the Saint Lawrence for two days and, word has it, we're now on the Ottawa River. The one that will take me to Bytown. To Annie.

"The captain says it's up there on the left, just around the bluff," Billy says, coming to join us.

"I hardly know how the captain got a word in edgewise," Joe chides. "Sure, you talked the poor man's ears off!"

"And how am I to learn if not by asking?" Billy says. "I was born this handsome, but do you think I was born this brilliant?"

"Billy," Joe looks at him sideways. "You're about as brilliant as a mud puddle and as handsome as its wallowing sow."

But Billy isn't one to be put off. "Well, when I make my fortune here in Upper Canada, 'twill be money I'm rolling in, you may be sure. And there's nothing more handsome than a rich man."

"Rolling in money?" Joe teases. I have to laugh, for Billy has nothing but the ragged clothes upon his back. "Have you forgotten where you came from, boy? We're Irish, and poor Irish at that. Don't be filling your head with such nonsense."

"The captain says many Irish have made their fortunes here in Upper Canada. Politicians and businessmen. Barons of land and lumber. Imagine that, Kit. Me, a baron." He tucks his thumbs in his armpits and stares off into the wooded shore drifting by us. "Just like Nicholas Sparks."

"Who?" I ask.

"Don't encourage him," Joe moans, rolling his eyes as Billy grins, excited to have an audience.

"Nicholas Sparks. The captain said Mr. Sparks came here from Ireland thirty years back. Right off the boat, so he was, young Nick." Billy's eyes are aglow. He's a fair storyteller, that Billy. I could well imagine him sitting by the fire weaving tales. "Nick starts working as a farmhand for a wealthy man named Wright."

"So? Sure, that's no different than in Ireland," Joe says, as hooked as a gaping cod.

"*So*," Billy continues with a knowing grin, "five years later, Nick's earned enough to buy himself *two hundred acres*."

"Two hundred?" I blurt. "B'jaysus, that's the size of Killanamore town!"

"... *and*," Billy continues, "he married Wright's widowed daughter-in-law. They live in a grand stone house in Bytown."

I can almost see the waterwheel turning in the currents of Billy's thoughts. If Nick Sparks can do it, anyone can. Maybe the Canadas really are different than back home. Billy's enthusiasm spreads as quickly as the fever. Soon I'm as excited about it as he is.

"Sounds like the captain said a lot of things," Joe mutters; he sounds annoyed. "Did he tell you about the canal?" He nods at the stone locks appearing in the dusk light as we round the bluff. Six giant steps cut the cleft, climbing to an arched bridge at the hilltop. "That's the start of miles and miles of canal. Did he tell you how many Irishmen met their death digging it for the British soldiers?"

I shudder, suddenly chilled at the thought of my Da and all

the other men who died on the road works back home. Billy doesn't speak.

"Did he tell you about the French?" Joe continues. He scowls as though the words taste bad upon his tongue. He's not enjoying what he has to say. "About how they hate the Irish for coming here and taking their jobs? Did he?"

"No," Billy mumbles.

"How do you know all this, Joe?" I ask. For he'd not said a word about it the whole way over.

"My uncles came and worked on the canal with Grandad's brother. Grandad never talked about it much. He didn't want them to leave Ireland."

"I thought his brother worked in the lumber camps," I say, remembering the day Murph told me that in the ship's hold.

Joe nods and leans his folded arms on the rail. "After the canal was built, his brother Daniel got work as a cook in a lumber camp, but my two uncles wouldn't go with him. They stayed in Bytown." He takes a deep breath. "And died in Bytown."

"The fever?" Billy asks.

"A bullet. Both of them shot dead in riots on the streets of

Bytown." He clenches his jaw and turns his back to the locks.

"Killed for being Irish."

CHAPTER TWENTY-EIGHT

We don't talk as the steamer moors at the base of the locks, each of us lost in our thoughts. What sort of a place is Bytown, I wonder, for it sounds like both hell and heaven on earth. Stepping onto the wharf, fat rain taps our shoulders, reminding us it's time to go home, reminding us we have no home to go to.

"Joe! Brigid!" a man shouts, waving madly as he climbs out of a wagon. In the fading light, I mistake him for Murph at first. He's a Murphy, all right, Murphy's son. Brigid charges for her father, who catches her and throws her in the air just like Da used to do with me. My eyes sting at the sight of their reunion, at the reminder of my loss. Joe, Billy, and I walk over to join them as

Joe's father looks past us onto the ship, looking for his wife and youngest daughter. For his father, Murph.

"They didn't make it, Da," Joe says, his voice soft. He stares at the dirt road. "Mam and Mary, they caught the fever and ..."

Grief pools in Mr. Murphy's eyes as he rests his hand on Joe's shoulders, the shoulders that bore the burden all this way.

"... and Grandad caught the fever at Grosse Isle," Joe ends.

"I'm sorry for your loss, Mr. Murphy," I say. "I knew your father. He was a great man, God rest him."

"I wish he'd the strength for the journey," Joe's da answers. "But he got you here safe and sound, didn't he?" He hugs Brigid and claps his arms around Joe. After all he's lost, what is found is all the more precious.

Mr. Murphy looks at Billy and me and wipes his eyes. "We haven't much, but you're both welcome to stay with us in Richmond until you get your feet under you," he says, so like his father before him. "There's room in the barn loft."

"Thanks, just the same," I answer, even though my body feels like it could sleep for days on end. As inviting as a bed of hay sounds, I haven't come all this way to quit now. "But I'm looking for my sister."

"And I'm off to see the town," Billy says, and before any of us can stop him, he's up the path and into the shadows.

"Well, the door is always open at our place if you're in need," Mr. Murphy says as I hug Brigid goodbye. Hand in hand they head back to the wagon.

"Won't you come with us, Kit?" Joe asks. "This isn't a place for a lost girl."

"That's why I've to find my Annie," I answer. "Don't worry about me; I'll be fine."

He seems unconvinced. "Well, you know where I am if you need me," he says. "After all we've been through, you're like a brother to me … or sister."

We laugh. I want him to stay. I need his strength more than ever. I don't want to be alone. Again.

"Go on, now," I say hugging him quickly and pushing him away. "Your da is waiting."

They climb into the wagon and set off home. Joe waves as they climb the dirt road up the side of the hill. And then they're gone.

Home. Will I ever have one again?

The rain falls harder, muddying the banks of the river where I stand with a hundred others. Though the June air presses heavy and humid around me, I can't stop shivering. We line the bank of the river like abandoned cargo. Men, women, children. Old and young. Most of us still sick from the fever and the journey. Survivors.

We've arrived. We made it. But where? What now?

I know no one. I have nothing. Nothing but a few coins from Father McGauran, a rosary I'll never pray, and the dirty clothes on my back. Rags that aren't even mine, truth be told, for I'd stolen them as a disguise all those long weeks back. Only ten weeks but, good Lord, it feels like another lifetime.

Scraps of family huddle together; others just lie down where they are to wait for help or death. I wrap my arms tight around me, trying to hold myself together. In clothes that make me someone I'm not, in the shadow of a town that's not my home, I know only one thing for sure.

I've never felt so lost.

CHAPTER TWENTY-NINE

Not long after we arrive, five robed figures emerge from the shadows. Each one carries a basket and bucket. As they draw nearer, I notice they all wear the same dress: a long brown robe, a black bonnet, a black squared cowl like a bib draped over their front and back. From their dress and their big silver crosses glinting in the lanterns' light, they must be nuns.

Behind them follows a girl a bit older than me in a long purple dress, white cowl, and bonnet, and a tall man carrying a medical bag. He stops and kneels by a little girl lying in the mud. By the way he touches her forehead and throat I know he's a doctor. The doctor says something and the girl in the purple dress gently lifts the child and carries her to a wagon waiting on the path back in the shadows.

The shortest of the nuns approaches me. She's young, not yet thirty, I'd say; still there's something in her gray eyes that makes me think she's older. A wise soul, Mam would have said.

"Bread, son?" she asks, dropping her bundles and kneeling beside where I sit, heedless to the drizzle and mud. She hands me a hunk of bread and pours a cup of milk from the jug within her basket. I'd never tasted anything so good. Wrapping a blanket around my shoulders, she rubs my back gently like Mam would. The tenderness of it makes me cry.

"You have journeyed long, *oui*?" she says, gently touching my forehead, checking me for signs of the fever.

I nod.

"You miss your home?" She looks around and realizes I'm alone. "Your family, *mon cher*?" But I don't need to answer. Her eyes read my very heart.

Taking a cloth, she wets it in the bucket and begins washing arms and legs, rinsing away all the filth from the journey. Her chapped hands are surprisingly gentle as she washes my face. She wrings the cloth and hangs it on the bucket lip before lathering soap in my hair. I close my eyes as she combs my curls, stopping her rhythmic strokes every now and then to pick out the lice as I had done for Jack on Grosse Isle.

"I will cut this shorter for you." She pulls out a pair of scissors. "It will be easier to keep it clean and free from pests."

I nod, not bothering to tell her I'm a girl. The other robed women are doing the same for other immigrants, combing and cutting hair, washing bodies, shaving the men. Such simple things, really, but it amazes me how wonderful it feels. To be clean. To be cared for.

"Are you French?" I ask, for I recognize her accent. It sounds like some I'd heard on Grosse Isle.

"*Oui*, from Montreal," she says, continuing to comb my hair. "I, too, left my home and family. But Bytown is my home now."

"Why are you helping me?" I ask, thinking of what Joe said about the French and Irish in Bytown. "I'm Irish."

She stops brushing and turns me to face her, her gray eyes stern. I'm sorry I asked.

"Irish, French, what does it matter, mon fils? We are all God's children. We are family. I hope that you would do the same for me."

I don't answer, for truth be told, I doubt I would.

She pulls a new pair of pants and a clean shirt from her basket. "*Tiens*, put these on." She motions for me to change behind a row of bushes.

When I come back, she takes my dirty shirt and pants and moves on to tend to the other immigrants further down the bank. Giving clean clothes and fresh food. Giving her time and attention. Giving dignity.

An upturned rowboat lies on the bank, propped against a boulder. Not wanting to get my fresh clothes wet from the rain, I crawl underneath. A few small children come and join me, tucking their muddy feet under them as we watch the nuns move from person to person, until all are visited.

"Mother Bruyere," the girl in the purple dress calls and the short woman turns. I hadn't realized she was the Mother of the order. "Doctor Van Cortlandt has sent the worst patients to the hospital. But it's full now and the sheds are not finished." She looks around at the immigrants. About two dozen of us, the healthier ones, if you could call us that, are left. "What are we to do?"

"Martha," Mother Bruyere answers. "We shall have to make the best with what we have." She glances around and, seeing us under the boat, smiles. "See? The Lord always provides."

CHAPTER THIRTY

I rise with the sun, eager to start my search for Annie, anxious to get out from under the stuffy boat, where five of us huddled to keep dry last night. My back cracks like kindling as I stand and stretch, taking in the landscape. Other than trees and water, there isn't much to see down at the river's edge, but a quick climb up the path by the locks brings me atop the arched bridge.

So this is Bytown.

The canal continues from under the bridge, splitting the town in two. Buildings of all sizes cluster on either side of the canal banks like women at the market. Further ahead, the canal loops into a small bay edged by warehouses, mills, and moored barges and boats. The banter of workmen unloading barrels and bags drifts to me on a hops and barley breeze. A brewery, no doubt, which doesn't surprise me, given the number of taverns lining the canal.

Bytown is much bigger than I expected, at least a hundred Killanamores. Finding someone in Bytown is going to be difficult—good news when it comes to hiding from Henry Lynch, for I've no doubt he's out there on the hunt, too. Still, it's bad news when it comes to my search for Annie. I glance at both halves of the town, unsure of where to start.

Great stone buildings stand on the right at the upper end of the bridge. They're much bigger than any of our cottages in Killanamore, though not as grand as the Big House. Men in suits and black bowler hats travel the planked walkways. At first, I think they're landlords, but there are so many. Surely they can't all be landlords.

It's as though the bridge spans two different towns, for down to the left end of the bridge is surely a working man's world. Farmers' wagons travel the muddy roads that crisscross lower town like a dirt tartan. Two men tie their horses' reins to the hitching post and, brushing the dust from their breeches, head into the harness maker's shop. I can't read the lettered names over the windows, but even I know a blacksmith from a baker. I've only to look at the picture on the sign hanging out front. Grocers, hotels, chemists, saloons, furriers, saddlers, and that's just on this corner of town. Squealing draws my eyes to the muddy ditch where two muck-splattered boys grapple with a slippery pig rooting in the street's garbage. Their antics remind me of Mick and Jack, making me smile, making me wince. *Will I ever see Jack and Mick again?*

"Kit!" Billy calls from the other side of the bridge. His eyes are sparkling with excitement as he crosses to meet me, dodging the wagons and carriages. "Isn't Bytown brilliant?" he asks, breathless. "Wait until you see! I spent the night just wandering up and down the roads. B'jaysus, there's a lot of them. But you've got to see this first! Come on!"

Grabbing my wrist, he pulls me to the right, to the upper part of town.

"Slow down, Billy!" I call, for he's near running now, and me clattering behind. We'll surely end up in a heap, the pair of us, or run over by a cart, for there's many on the road even at this early hour. He stops outside a two-storey stone house and stands in the street looking up at it. We don't dare let our dirty feet mar the planked walkway running before it.

"This is it!" Billy says, like we've found the Holy Grail.

"Is Annie here?" I ask, suddenly excited. Maybe he'd spent the night looking for her. I should have gone with him.

"Who?" He looks back at the house. "No. Sure, this is the very home of Nicholas Sparks. He lives here, Kit. And some day, I'm going to have a house just like it."

"Move along there, you pair!" A man in a suit waves his cane at us as he approaches the house. "You've no business in Upper Town." He stops and opens the gate.

"Are you Mr. Sparks, sir?" Billy calls, as bold as brass.

The man stops. "I am Mr. Miller. Not that it is any of your concern."

"Well, Mr. Miller, would you be so kind as to tell Mr. Sparks that Billy—I mean, Mr. William Farrell—would like to meet him?"

My mouth drops. Leave it to Billy. Sure, he'd ask for one thread and shear the whole sheep.

Mr. Miller walks up to Billy and lowers his voice. "Listen, messenger boy. I don't know what sort of man your boss is, but you may tell Mr. Farrell that the civilized book appointments at the office and not through the bellowing of street urchins." His scornful gaze makes me stare down at my muddy feet. Even my new clothes leave me feeling shameful.

"Yessir," Billy exclaims. "I'll surely tell him. My boss, that is. Mr. Farrell." He lifts his hand and speaks behind it as if letting Mr. Miller in on a big secret. "He's only off the boat, you see. He still has a lot to learn."

Mr. Miller shakes his head. "Lower Town scum," he mutters, slamming the gate shut behind him.

"Hungry?" Billy asks me, totally unfazed by the whole thing.

I nod and he leads the way back down to the bridge.

"You're not planning on making an appointment with Mr. Sparks, are you?" I ask. He can't be serious.

"And why not?" Billy says, with that grin of his.

He flabbergasts me, so he does. But he's looking at me, waiting for an answer.

"Well … you can't just … you're a …" I stammer but the

words are slippery as eels.

"I'm a poor, illiterate, Irish immigrant?" Billy says for me.

"Well, yes!" I laugh.

"So was Nicholas Sparks and dozens of other men just like him."

"But Billy, you have to know your limits."

He stops on the bridge and turns to me, his face serious. "Says who?"

I shrug. Lynch said it to me a few times when I was working in the Big House. But everyone knows. It's the way of things. Everyone has their place. "'Tis common sense, Billy."

"I had a dog," he interrupts, "by the name of Cullen. Oh, he was a cracker of a thing. Smart as a whip—you could learn him anything, but he had a bit of wolf in him, so he did. Da didn't want him running away so he trained him. Taught him to mind the boundaries of our farm. Day after day he'd walk Cullen around the farm limits and discipline him to never step foot off that property. Whipped him if he did. But Cullen knew there were great adventures beyond those limits. He could smell them." His eyes stare off into memory. In all our time together, Billy never spoke of where he came from, of his family or past. He looks at me, serious again.

"Limits are manmade things, Kit. Things other people invent to hold us back. 'Tis up to us to bide them or not."

He has a point. Sure, haven't I crossed many the line in the past year? Not just farm limits and county lines, but even theft and murder.

He raises his arm, taking in the town. "Imagine a world without limits, Kit. Imagine the freedom and the opportunities there for the taking! For any man … or woman!" he adds. "That's what Bytown is."

"It sounds lawless," I say, leery of a town like that. "Wild."

"Exactly!" Billy flashes his smile. "And aren't wolves made for running in the wild?"

And right there, on the bridge straddling Upper and Lower Town, in the space between the wealthy and working man's worlds, that cheeky pup, Billy Farrell, let out a howl.

CHAPTER THIRTY-ONE

Stall after stall of fruit, baked goods, fresh meat, and fish, the By Ward Market has it all. Farmers' carts trundle down the muddy roads to line up along the double-wide street while men and women stop, laden baskets in hand, to catch up on neighbors' news. 'Tis like a county fair. And Billy says this happens every day.

I follow him to a busy stall and hide behind another cart. We've made our plan. He's to cause a distraction while I grab and run, but my stomach is in knots from nerves and hunger. Had I any other choice, I'd take it.

Right on cue, Billy pulls a few apples from the bottom of the mound, causing the whole thing to spill to the ground. Billy bolts, apples in hand, while the farmer's wife tries to reign in the rolling fruit.

It's now or never.

Bursting from my hiding spot, I snatch two fresh loaves from the other corner of their stall but, just as I'm about to run, something grabs the back of my neck.

"Steal from me, will you, you Irish brat!" The farmer's got me. He shakes me by the scruff like a hound with a mewling kitten. His grip is like an iron bite and no matter how I kick and squirm, there's no breaking free. "I've had enough of you lot! Time I made an example of one of you."

He drags me into the road. I've no idea what punishment he's got in mind and, from the look in his eye, no desire to find out. Three brown robes catch my eye at a stall across the street. One holds out her basket, nodding her black-bonneted head as a man drops in a few vegetables from his cart.

"Mother Bruyere!" I cry out, hoping it's her. "Help me, please!"

She turns and sees me staggering alongside the angry farmer. Motioning for her sisters to stay, she crosses into the street to join us.

"Monsieur Desjardins," her voice is strong and clear. She reaches into her pocket and holds out two coins. "I believe this will pay for the boy's bread and a little more for your trouble."

He hesitates before taking them. Were it not Mother Bruyere offering, I've no doubt he would have chosen vengeance and violence over payment, but everyone is watching now. Instead, he throws me to my hands and knees on the muddy road.

"I better not catch you anywhere near my stall!" He points his thick farmer's finger at me. "Do you hear me, boy?"

"Yessir," I mumble. The loaves lay in a mud puddle beside me, their crusts mangled from my clenched fingers, though my neck be in worse shape. It throbs from where he'd gripped, and I reach up to assure myself that his hand is truly gone. After a few moments, the crowds go back to their early morning shopping, but Mother Bruyere still stands before me.

"Thank you," I say, looking up from the muddied hem of her robe. I sit back on my heels and rub my neck. "You—you saved my life."

"And you waste it," she says, her gray eyes like a winter sky, her voice cold. The other two sisters have come to join her. "We beg for donations to feed the immigrants, to feed your people. Do you think Mr. Desjardins is going to be charitable now?"

"I'm sorry, Mother," I say, for I truly am, though I can't ever imagine Mr. Desjardins as charitable, even on a good day.

"I am not the one that needs to hear your confession," she continues. "But Father Molloy would." Her black bonnet nods at the stone church a few streets over, towering behind the houses, overlooking all of Lower Town. Seen from everywhere and seeing everything.

I stare back at the ground. Apologizing to her is one thing. Apologizing to God himself is another thing entirely. Even though I'm on my knees, I'm not ready for that.

"Thank you for paying for the bread," I say, changing the subject. If they are begging for donations, I imagine they don't have much money.

"Do not thank me. Those were your coins. I found them in your pockets."

My stomach sinks. I need that money for when I find Annie, but I suppose I deserve what I get.

Pulling some clothes from her basket, Mother Bruyere drops

them in front of me. I barely recognize them as my own, for they're washed, the holes patched, the tattered hems re-stitched.

"You fixed them—but why?" I ask, knowing she must have sewn by candlelight well into the night. "They were just rags."

"A little washing, a little mending, and now they are new again," the youngest sister answers, and I see her basket is full of clothing. "Just like our souls."

Mother Bruyere holds out Father Robson's black rosary.

"It isn't mine," I say. "I was holding it for Father Robson at Grosse Isle," I quickly add, for fear she'd think I'd stolen it. But she keeps her hand out. The silver cross dangles from the end of the black beads. It reminds me of Mam, of all the times we knelt by our hearth, the five of us, praying the rosary together. As much as I disliked it at the time, I'd give anything to be a bored daughter at family prayer and not an orphaned thief kneeling in the muddy streets of Bytown.

"I don't use it," I admit, ashamed. I won't take it from her. "You should give it to someone who needs it."

"I am," she says, laying it on top of the clothes pile.

I wait for her to leave me, to wash her hands of me, but she doesn't move.

"This is not who I am," I mumble. Mam would have been so disappointed to see me like this, a faithless soul caught stealing. I take a deep breath and look up at the three sisters. "This isn't me."

Mother Bruyere's eyes soften.

"I just want to find my little sister, Annie," I say. "I just want to save my family. What's left of it." Though even that sounds hopeless, for I can't even feed myself.

"Sister Thibodeau," Mother Bruyere asks, "what does St. Benedict tell us?"

"Begin again," the nun with the small round glasses answers.

"And so we shall." Mother Bruyere gives me her hand and helps me stand. "Let's start with your name."

I look into her eyes and hesitate for a moment. But then I know deep in my heart, if I can trust anyone, 'tis her.

"I'm Kathleen," I say. "Kathleen Byrne."

"*Une fille?*" the youngest sister whispers, taking in the state of me, a short-haired, muddied thief in pants. Not quite what you'd expect from a young lady, but Mother Bruyere smiles. As though she knows. As though she sees some worth in the rag of a soul before her.

"*Viens*, Kathleen," Mother Bruyere says. "If your Annie is in Bytown, I know just how to find her."

CHAPTER THIRTY-TWO

Mother Bruyere knocks on doors in Upper and Lower Town all morning. I half hope she will ask about Annie's whereabouts at the next door, but she doesn't. All she asks for are food donations, just as her companions do in other parts of town. Most folk add something to her baskets: bread, cheese, some vegetables. One woman has a hot bucket of broth waiting for us. By the time the summer sun sits high overhead, my arms are aching with the weight of bucket and basket. I feel as laden as Squib, our poor oul' donkey back home.

How much food do nuns eat?

I lug my burdens back over the bridge into Lower Town,

following Mother Bruyere down an alleyway and into a ramshackle boarding house. The place stinks like a workhouse. We climb to the top floor, stopping outside a dilapidated door. Surely she doesn't think anyone here would have donations. Knocking, she lets herself in.

The place is near empty, save for a worn stool, a cold pot in a fireless hearth, and a family huddled in the dark corner. 'Tis a mother and two children resting on a thin, straw mattress. The mother smiles as we enter and tries to rise, but hasn't the strength.

"Easy, Agnes." Mother Bruyere is at her side, cupping the woman's head, gently lowering it. "Save your energy."

"I haven't even the strength to put on the kettle and offer my visitors a cup of tea," Agnes says, her Irish accent steeped in regret.

"Hush, now." Mother Bruyere wipes the hair from Agnes's sweaty face and takes her hand. "Don't worry about that. Besides, we aren't visitors. We are family."

Relieved to finally set down the bucket and basket, I roll my aching shoulders. The older of the two children, a girl of about eight, leaves her mother and comes to stand before me. Her younger brother follows close behind, curious about this new visitor.

"Are you my family, too?" the girl says shyly.

I look at Mother Bruyere and then back at the shadowed eyes in the wan face before me. I don't even know her name, but I know her life. I know she's carried the burden of care on her bony shoulders—a burden she can neither carry nor lay down. I wish I could help her, but I can't. Aren't I yoked enough by my own troubles? I look away.

"I always wanted an older brother," the boy says, stepping forward, eyes pleading. "Can you be him?"

"I'm a girl," I say, avoiding his question.

Their look of surprise makes me laugh. "Things aren't always what they seem."

"That's what Theresa always says, don't you?" The brother looks up at her. Theresa nods.

"You can't tell by looking at us," he continues, his tongue lisping in his gap-toothed grin, "but we're descendants of the King himself."

"My Da used to tell me that, too," I murmur. The memory of it stings.

"So we *are* family ... we're all the king's descendants, right,

Theresa?"

She nods but her somber eyes tell me she no longer believes, either.

Mother Bruyere pulls a blanket from the basket by my feet and nods at the bucket. "The children are hungry."

Finding a few tin cups by the cold fireplace, I kneel and scoop from the bucket. The least I can do is give them broth. Lukewarm it is, but by the way they guzzle it, I suppose that's best. I refill their cups and hand them a bit of bread.

"A carrot and three potatoes!" the boy cries out, as though he's found buried treasure at the bottom of his cup. Though my shoulder still aches, I wish there were more vegetables in the bucket for him.

"Do you know any stories?" he asks.

I know hundreds, but truth be told, I don't want to tell any. They remind me of Da, of sitting 'round our hearth, of us all being together. Just thinking about it makes my chest ache.

"Hush, Frankie!" Theresa scolds like a wee mam, reading the expression on my face. "She brought you soup, didn't she? Just be thankful for that."

Frankie slumps and fiddles with his bread. So like Jack. I know he's as starving for a good yarn.

"I know a few," I admit. And so I begin. "Let me tell you of a tale, not your time, nor mine ..." Da's voice echoes in my head and words. I take a deep breath, then another as the ache comes. But this time when I close my eyes, I see neither the wagon that brought him home that rainy night nor the grave where his body rests. I see him. I see Da. He's sitting in his chair, his face half lit by the firelight. I weave his words, mimicking everything from the lilt of his voice to the wave of his hands, for I know it all by heart. It seems so real, I can almost feel our fire's heat on my face, almost hear the logs snap and shift when he pauses. I take a breath and feel no ache as my nose is filled with the scent of fresh-cut hay, lye soap, and pipe tobacco. The smell of Da.

"And there she lies to this very day. Or so the story goes," I end, slowly opening my eyes, almost surprised to find I'm in a small, dark room and not back home. The two children gathered around me lean in, hearts warmed, faces flushed, and eyes sparkling as though I were a fire myself.

Frankie claps. "That was brilliant! Do you know any Wild

Geese stories?"

"Wild Geese?" I snap, for I know the stories well enough; weren't they Jack's favorites? The Wild Geese were Irishmen who fought in European armies over hundreds of years ago. With a head full of that foolishness, is it any wonder he's chasing some silly dream of adventure instead of staying with his family? I glare at Frankie. "Why in God's name would you want to be hearing about that?"

Frankie shrugs. "Battles, great adventures, and glory."

My lips tighten. "What glory is there in leaving your homeland? What glory is there in battles fought on foreign soil, I ask you?"

Frankie looks down at his cold broth.

"Don't be filling your head with such nonsense," I scold. But he has to know. Someone has to set him straight. "They'll give you nothing but foolish ideas, Jack."

"Jack?" Frankie asks, looking up at me. "Who's Jack?"

CHAPTER THIRTY-THREE

When we say our goodbyes, the children ask me to come back and tell more stories. I promise to, though I doubt I will. What good are stories anyway? Look what they did for Jack. Stories don't fill bellies, and that's the sorry truth of it.

We travel the dirty roads further into Lower Town, carefully navigating the wagon ruts baked hard by the hot sun. I'd already tripped over them a few times, nearly spilling the rest of the soup. Soup that had to feed many more families like Agnes's.

"Has Agnes the fever?" I ask, though I know well enough.

Mother Bruyere nods. "Typhus. It is spreading in Bytown. The sheds we are building will be ready in a day or two, but even those cannot hold the numbers I foresee. Already our hospital is full and more steamers are heading this way."

We walk in silence. I wonder if Agnes will live. I wonder what will happen to Theresa and Frankie then.

We visit family after family that afternoon, giving out our collected food. They are so grateful to get it that I feel bad for complaining about the weight. When we reach the bottom of the basket, my only wish is that there had been more to give, for it seems there are needy, hungry, and sick families all over Lower Town.

As we travel, I begin to learn the names of the Lower Town streets: Rideau, George, York, where the market is, Sussex, and, of course, Sappers Bridge, linking Upper and Lower Town. Down Clarence Street, a small crowd has gathered around a fight outside a hotel. I can scarce believe my eyes when I see 'tis two women brawling, pulling each other's hair and ripping at their already scanty clothes. A few rough-looking men lean on posts, sharing swigs from a bottle, laughing at the women's display. A drunken man staggers into the fray.

"Girls, girls," he drawls. "There's enough of me for both of you." But a punch from the dark-haired one lands him flat on his back.

Billy is right about one thing, I think as we hurry past. *This place is wild.*

"Someone should call the police," I whisper to Mother Bruyere, for, in truth, the dark-haired woman, a girl, really, could only be a year older than me.

"There are no police," she answers, picking up her pace.

"But what about the soldiers?" I ask, for I've seen some up on Barrack Hill; they were posted on the Upper Town bluff by the canal locks.

"They came to build the Rideau Canal and stayed in case the Americans attack."

"So they're protecting the canal?" I ask in disbelief. "Good Lord! Then who's protecting us?"

She looks back at me and smiles. "The good Lord."

As we walk up Sussex Street, I see Sister Thibodeau returning from her day's work. She looks as tired as I feel, but she smiles and greets us as we round the corner at the huge stone church and stop outside three white, two-storey wooden houses tucked in just behind it. Mother Bruyere tells me they are a convent where the sisters live, a boarding house, and a hospital.

"Mother Bruyere," Sister Thibodeau says, pushing up her glasses. "I will check on the patients here before stopping by the hospital." I notice then that she is carrying a small black doctor's bag.

"Are you a healer?" I ask.

"Sister Thibodeau knows much about medicine," Mother Bruyere says, proud of her sister's talent. "I don't know where we'd be without her."

But not basking in the praise, Sister Thibodeau is already at the hospital door.

"Now, Kathleen," Mother Bruyere says, stopping outside the boarding house. "We have one more task before our day is done."

I just want to sit and rest; my arms ache; my feet are throbbing. I've done penance and a half for the bit of bread I stole, but I nod at her request.

She smiles. "Follow me, *ma chère*."

Opening the door to the boarding house, she calls to the

young lady inside. It is the girl from the canal, the one wearing a long, plain, purple dress.

"*Martha, on cherche sa petite soeur. Où sont les filles?*"

"*Oui, Mère,*" Martha answers, coming from the back room. She waves us in. *"Elles lavent la vaisselle."*

I've no idea what they are saying, but Martha smiles at me and points to the back room.

Mother Bruyere leads me to a small kitchen where a dozen girls of all ages clean up. One sweeps with a broom, another wipes the long table and benches where they must have just eaten, and the rest dry the dishes being washed by a little blonde girl with ringlets just like—

"Annie?" I whisper, afraid to believe it. It looks like her, a shadow of her, really, for she'd lost even more weight over these long weeks. She pulls her soapy hands from the basin as she turns, her arms and legs like thin spindles. She peers at me from above dark smudges in her pale face. Annie, but not all of her. She's lost a bit of herself on the journey. I suppose we all have. "Annie?" I kneel and reach out to touch her. "Is it you? Is it really you?"

Her eyes hold no recognition, as though they've seen enough

these long months.

"Annie, it's me, love. Kit."

"Annie doesn't talk," says the little redhead with the dishtowel. I realize it's Tish Crean, her friend from Ireland. If Tish is here, then she must be an orphan, too, God rest her parents. What have these poor girls been through, I wonder.

I wrap my arms around Annie. She seems so fragile. Still, it feels good to hold her again. Her wet hands slowly circle my waist, soaking the back of my shirt, squeezing tighter and tighter. "I found you, Annie. I found you," I whisper into her hair. "Everything is going to be all right now."

"God listens," Tish said. "Annie prayed right hard, so she did. Every day on the boat she asked God to watch over you. And here you are, safe and sound."

"But, Kit," Tish says looking around the floor behind me. "Where's the puppy she prayed for?"

CHAPTER THIRTY-FOUR

After my reunion with Annie, I don't want to leave her, but Mother Bruyere tells me I'm too old to stay with the orphans. As it turns out, Father Molloy has just opened a new place on Church Street, Saint Raphael House, for girls my age. "It's the perfect place to help you get back on your feet again," she says. "There are a few girls living there now, mostly Irish. Perhaps you will find a friend."

I don't bother telling her 'tis money I need, not friendship.

The house is tiny and a bit of a shambles. Even the inside looks fit for rats and mice, truth be told. Though I suppose orphaned, pauper teenage girls aren't worth much more.

"*Marie*?" Mother Bruyere calls to a girl tending a small fire in the darkened room. "*Voici Kathleen, une immigrante nouvelle. Donne-lui des vêtements.*"

Marie looks at my boyish appearance questioningly but nods and leaves the room.

"A girl?" an Irish voice asks. I see a dark-haired girl looking me over, her arms folded. Two more girls stand behind her.

"Yes," Mother Bruyere answers. "Rose, I expect you to show Kathleen the same charity you have received."

Rose smiles, but the flickering firelight, her face seemed almost evil. "Of course, Mother."

Mother Bruyere shows me to the upstairs room where five sparse beds are crammed. "This one is yours," the nun says, nodding at the bed under the window. Marie returns with a pile of neatly folded items and hands them to me. Blankets, a nightdress, skirts and tops, shoes. "All donations from the Ladies of Charity," Mother Bruyere says. "Everything in this house is a gift given out of the generosity of others."

My eyes roam the dingy room, the mouse scurrying in the corner. I clutch the pile of clothes, knowing I should be grateful.

"While you live in this house and look for work, all donations of food or clothing are equally shared among the girls," Mother Bruyere says to me. It sounds fair, but the way Marie cowers at Rose's glare makes me think differently. "Room and board, clothing, training for domestic work, Saint Raphael House is here to help you help yourself."

Mother Bruyere bids us goodnight but, as she leaves, an uneasiness scurries in the corners of my mind. As soon as the front door closes, Rose turns on me.

"I'll take that!" she says, snatching the blankets and shoes while the others rummage through my meager pile.

"But—" I say, as the words are slapped from my mouth.

"Shut your gob!" Rose says. "You're in *my* house now." The other two girls laugh.

"Let me tell you the *real* rules, shall I?" Rose continues. "I don't cook or clean for nobody. Not some high and mighty Upper Town snot and definitely not for some poor culchie girl, like you."

"Are you sure 'tis a girl?" one of the two asks from the shadows, as a hand reaches out and tweaks my breast. I cry out and slap it away. "Sure, she's as flat as a plank."

"Aye, Norah, but she cries like a little girl."

More laughter.

Rose steps in closer, backing me into the corner of the tiny room. "I get first dibs here, Kathleen. Anything that comes through that door, any bit of food or clothing, or work, 'tis mine for the taking or leaving." She pokes me hard. "Understand?"

I nod, even though I know she can barely see me in the darkened room.

"Well, then, welcome to Saint Raphael House," she proclaims. "The ideal place to help me help myself."

"Good one, Rose," a voice chuckles.

"Sheila, leave the dress," Rose orders over her shoulder. "We can't have The Goose suspecting anything, now, can we?" It lands in a heap at my feet.

Rose turns back to face me, stepping in close. "Go crying to Mother Bruyere, Sister Phelan, or Father Molloy," she lowers her voice, "and you'll find yourself floating face down in the canal."

No one laughs. Evidently, this threat is no joke.

They leave the room and I slump in the corner on the thin pallet. The tiny mattress is near emptied of all its straw, pilfered no doubt by Rose and her cronies. I've no blankets, but the night is warm. Besides, now that I've found Annie, I plan on being long gone by the time the autumn chill comes. We'll get some money and get a place of our own. Bundling the dress under my head, I lay back and look at the moon's clipping as it shines through the dirty window. The same moon I studied through the window of my cell in Wicklow Jail.

I survived that hell, I tell myself. *The famine, the jail, the crossing. I found Jack. I found Annie. I will survive this.*

I will.

Someday, I'll be looking at that moon through the window of my own home with my family gathered 'round. There is a way; there has to be, even if I can't see it yet.

I stare at the sliver of light and just beyond to where its heavenly body is swallowed in shadow.

Just because I can't see it doesn't mean it isn't there.

CHAPTER THIRTY-FIVE

"Get up there, girls," a woman's voice calls as she rings a bell downstairs. The other girls grumble and pull their blankets over their heads. Slipping on my dress, the only item I've left from last night's raid, I leave the room and enter the small kitchen where Marie stirs a pot over the fire. Another woman—a nun, I can tell by the same brown habit they all wear—is emptying some items from her basket onto the rickety table: a loaf of bread, a jug of milk, some cheese, and three apples. My mouth waters at the sight.

"You must be Kathleen," she says to me. There's a hint of Irish in her voice. "I'm Sister Phelan." She looks at my wrinkled dress. "Look at the state of you. Did you sleep in that, or what?" Her accent and tone remind me of Mam.

Marie glances at me and I see her dress is just as wrinkled. With no boy's clothes, I imagine she must have slept in hers. But before I can answer, Sister Phelan notices my bare feet.

"Where are your shoes, girl?" she asks me as Rose, Norah, and Sheila enter the room.

"Rose has them," I say.

Marie gasps and drops the spoon. It splatters porridge down her skirts. Rose glares at me from behind Sister Phelan; her dark eyes hit me like black stones from a slingshot.

"I never wore shoes back home," I lie. "They hurt my feet."

Sister Phelan shakes her head at me. "Well, you'll have to get used to them. You can't work Uptown in bare feet. I guess Rose will take that job. But Rose, try to keep this one. 'Tis the third job this month."

Rose smiles and grabs an apple. "Of course, sister."

Sighing, Sister Phelan takes the apple back and cuts it in half. She hands the other half to me. "Our last domestic just quit, Kathleen. The job is yours."

"A job?" I blurt. Amazed at how last night's problem of money is already solved. "A paying job?"

"'Tisn't much, but it's a start," Sister Phelan answers, picking up her basket. "You'll be helping Martha Hagan with the laundry. She's waiting for you at the boarding house."

"You couldn't pay me enough to do that filthy work," Rose mutters, ignoring the look from Sister Phelan. Rose cuts into the bread, letting a thick slice fall on the table. "You're welcome to it."

"Thanks, Rose," I say, taking the slice of bread and a bit of cheese to go with it. A bold move for sure, but hunger does that to me. Rose scowls, both of us knowing I'd have neither when Sister Phelan left. Not wanting to find out, I follow after Sister Phelan as she exits the tiny house.

I visit with Annie and Tish for a bit while waiting for Martha. Annie hasn't spoken to me yet; Tish speaks for her. Like peas in a pod, the pair of them. But Annie does sit with me and hold my hand. I even get a wee smile out of her before I have to leave with Martha.

"I take it you've done washing before?" Martha asks, handing me a bar of soap.

I nod, thinking fondly of doing the day's wash with Mam. I don't mind washing; besides, how dirty could sisters habits be?

She hands me one of the heaping baskets. I realize then it's the dirty rags of the immigrants. They stink to high heaven from weeks of wear, caked with filth, vermin, and God knows what. They should be burned, not washed. Just like that, my memory of Mam is gone, buried under dark and dingy memories of long days laundering uniforms in Wicklow Jail. That was my penance, my punishment for stealing. Yet, here I am again.

Martha leads me up St. Patrick Street, past the great stone cathedral, over the hill, and down to the water's edge. The early morning light dances on the Ottawa River as the thick woods around us rustle in the wind. A pretty scene; too bad it's for such dirty work.

Martha takes a bit of laundry and, kneeling, plunges into the river. Following her lead, I pull a filthy shirt from the basket but drop it quick, for 'tis speckled with nits and lice.

"This is disgusting," I say, flicking the few that jump up my arms. "I can see now why the last domestic quit."

"Do you think your clothes were any less dirty when Mother Bruyere washed them?" Martha asks with a smile as she wrings and plunges again.

"Why are we washing these rags anyway?" Taking a stick, I carry and plunge the infested rag into the river, drowning the little devils. "Sure, there'll be nothing but a collar and cuffs to hang with all the dirt gone."

"Think of it as prayer," Martha says.

Prayer? What sort of a church does she attend?

"Every sacrifice is one step closer to heaven," she explains.

I doubt that, but every rag *is* one step closer to buying a way out of here for Annie and me.

"Are you an orphan, too?" I ask. She seems about my age, and I wonder why she doesn't live at Saint Raphael's.

"No, my parents live in Bytown. My father is Hugh Hagan. He runs a private school on Sussex."

I know the school. I saw it yesterday in my travels.

"Hagan? So you're Irish, then?"

She nods. "My parents are from Derby County but I was born in Quebec."

"Are you a student at the school?" Mother Bruyere had mentioned her school yesterday, as well. It had to close while the sick immigrants took up all the sisters' time.

"I was," Martha says. "Soon, I'll be going to Montreal to do my novitiate studies. I'm a postulant," she explains, as though any of those words make sense to me. She gestures to her purple dress. "A sister in training."

I frown. 'Tis beyond me why anyone with a home and family, and a well-off one at that, would *choose* to leave them, choose this life of orphans, poverty, and illness, choose the very life I am trying to escape.

"There are a few postulants," Martha continues as she wrings and flicks the shirt in her hands before laying it on the branches to dry. She takes a pair of breeches and starts washing again. "When we make our novitiate vows, we get the habit the sisters wear."

She says it like it's a good thing. She is giving up everything I am working so hard to get. Is she mad?

"Oh, so you're not a sister yet," I say, dunking the shirt down for another rinse just to be sure. "You can still change your mind. That's good."

She stops scrubbing and sits back on her heels, looking at me like I'm the crazy one.

"Kit, doing this work makes me happy." She brushes a hair off her forehead with the back of her wrinkled, reddened hand. "It's where God wants me. Why would I say no?"

We stare at each other in confusion, two young girls side by side on the same shore, yet worlds apart.

CHAPTER THIRTY-SIX

I spend the next few weeks scrubbing rags on rocks and lugging baskets and buckets for Mother Bruyere. 'Tisn't really part of my job, but she wants me to come on some visits with her. She says it's good to see the faces of those I'm serving.

I don't see the point. I don't want to know them, don't want to hear that Agnes is doing worse. Haven't I enough of my own troubles without worrying about theirs? For one thing, after nearly a month of scouring, I've only red hands and a pittance of pennies to show for it. Even with the extra work Sister Phelan gave me cleaning the cathedral, I'll never get a home for Annie and me at this rate.

Can they not kneel without making such a mess? I polish this blasted banister every day, and every day 'tis covered in greasy handprints.

I run my rag along the worn wood, wiping away the fingerprints of the faithful. The altar rail curves around on the right end, around the statue of Our Lady. You'd never see that spot empty. Today a woman kneels deep in prayer before the rows of candles.

Like the Mother of God has nothing better to do than listen to those never-ending pleas. Like I've nothing better to do than clean those never-ending smudges.

A bit of polish on the rag helps, and, of course, a bit of elbow grease. After a few wipes, the wood shines as good as new as I move along to the right end. If only sin were so easy to clean. But my soul isn't just smudged, 'tis gouged by anger and bitterness. I'm still not sorry I tried to kill Lynch, only sorry it didn't work. I didn't even forgive Tom on his deathbed. I wanted him to suffer, like I had.

What kind of a person does that make me?

Mam always said that trials test our faith and make it stronger, just like how a pruned branch grows thicker. Mam, Da, and Jack. Mick. I miss them so. How much cutting back can one tree take before there's nothing left but a dead stump?

The woman mumbles as she slips the rosary through her fingers, bead by bead. I can well imagine Mam there, too. She would have loved this place, would have marveled at the great stone arches and smooth, carved pillars. Even I was amazed when I first entered those massive doors. Even I felt the power as I wandered up the aisle as wide and long as Sappers Bridge, to see Saint Patrick and Saint Jean-Baptiste like two sentinels, Irish and French, waiting at its end. In that moment, I felt Mam's awe.

But the statues and carvings, the windows and pews, the banisters and railings, they're just more things for me to clean, really. If I've learned anything, I know now that every church has its dirty corners. Bigger ones just have more.

Sister Phelan opens the poor box with the key on her belt. As promised, she hands me my wages and I drop them in my pocket. Martha may work for her heavenly reward, but I'll take the money, thanks very much. The coins jingle when I go back to buffing the railing. The praying woman shushes me, as though her muttering prayers are music to my ears. Still, I put one coin into my other empty pocket. 'Tisn't to please her sour puss, but the sound of money can only bring problems later. Especially if Rose hears it.

I don't keep my money at Saint Raphael's after Rose ransacked my bed a couple of times, looking for my pay. I tell her it's spent and she can't get blood from a stone, but she surely knows how to get it from my face. She's vicious, that one. Just last week, she snatched a loaf right from my hands as Father Molloy gave it to me from his basket. I grabbed it back only to have Norah and Sheila join in, all of us squawking and scratching, fighting like wild hens right there in front of Father Molloy. By the time he intervened, the loaf was flittered to crumbs, wasted from want. Father Molloy took off, basket and all, and wouldn't come back without Sister Phelan, who was none too pleased. She gave us a tongue lashing, so she did. Said she was ashamed of us, disgusted with our behavior. And in front of a priest, no less!

We stood there, heads hung, as she scolded us that night. I knew Sister Phelan's temper was getting the better of her. Her face grew redder with every wave of her arms. "What! Were!

You! Thinking!" she honked each word at us. I saw it then, why Rose calls Sister Phelan The Goose; those flapping sleeves, that gray-brown dress, the black bib and bonnet. I half expected her to stick out her neck, raise her arms, and come charging over the breadcrumbs at me. Oh, she was that riled.

Behind Sister Phelan's back, Rose stuck her thumbs in her armpits and flapped once. Well, that was it. The giggles came gurgling out of me. I knew I should stop; of all times to get a fit of tittering, of all people to be laughing at. Sister Phelan glared at me as I clapped my hand over my mouth, but I might as well try to stop a bubbling spring, for the sniggers spilled between my fingers and all over poor Sister Phelan. The other girls bit their smiles. Sister Phelan looked to heaven, as if to say, she's *your* daughter, then without another word, she turned on her heels and left. 'Twas a good thing she did, too. By the look in her eyes, if she'd stayed, if she'd spoken her mind, she'd be doing penance even longer than us.

The woman praying before the statue eyes me as I wipe nearer to her part of the railing. She glares as though she wants neither me nor my dirty rag near her. As though a rag's filth is its own fault. Doesn't she know? 'Tis the dirt of others that made it so.

Sister Phelan gave us a long lecture after the night we fought over the bread, spoke for ages about the way young ladies should behave. But we aren't ladies. We're Saint Raphael's girls. Not orphans. Not adults. We're nothing, really, and no amount of polishing can change what we are.

Hasn't she herself had a terrible time of finding us work? I used to think it was because we cannot read or write. But if the only quills a maid needs to know how to use are those feathers in a duster, why should I know how to read? For a while, I even thought it was because we were born in Ireland or baptized Catholic. Bytown's English and Scottish Protestants make it clear they don't want us around. They even challenge Mother Bruyere herself for helping us. Many of those Upper Town high and mighties are no different than our landlords back home.

But Rose spoke the bitter truth of it one night. "No one wants you," she said, trying to get a rise out of me. "You're bailed out of hell but barred from heaven. There's no place for you now, Kit. Who wants a Saint Raphael's girl? Be it the stink of sin or the scent of saintliness, you'll get neither love nor lust. You're a nothing. They should have just left you where they found you in the Clarence Street brothel."

I didn't correct her, for I realized then her harsh words were for herself. She doesn't scare me anymore. Like Ned Nowlan's dog back home, she's all bark, especially when someone's on her turf. Rose is right about one thing, though: folk avoid us. I've seen it. I've felt the stares and heard the whispers. Maybe they hate us because we're Catholic or Irish; maybe they judge us by what sins they think we've done or plan on doing; but I say they fear our misfortunes. 'Tis as though our shame were contagious.

The woman finally blesses herself and takes one last pleading look at Our Lady before leaving. Her candle flickers in its little glass, no different from the other dozens of prayers sputtering around it. The heat of them wafts into my face as I lean over to remove the gutted stubs from darkened cups. Martha and I will use them to make new candles. There must be about a hundred prayers burning before Our Lady. Yet, for all the light and warmth, my eyes are always drawn to those cups in shadow. The ones whose fire is long gone, the ones that hold nothing but cold, hardened leftovers.

It makes me wonder if anyone heard their melting pleas.

CHAPTER THIRTY-SEVEN

With chores done, I sneak up to my special place on the bluff across from the cathedral. I love it up here, above the laundresses' riverbank, above the town's prejudice and the church's check. Being up here helps me clear my head. When the dirt and dust of every day clogs my hope, I come up here and take hold of my future. A ratty wee sack half-full of coins.

Today's wages fall in, one lucky penny at a time, and my hope grows with each clink. But the good feeling doesn't last long. The bag is still half-empty. At this rate, Annie will be married by the time I've saved enough for us to start our home together.

I bury the sack back under a flat stone at the hilltop's edge and, settling myself on the great boulder in the middle of the bluff, stare out at the Ottawa River. 'Tis no ocean, but even so, there's something calming about watching it leave this town and head downstream, for I know it travels back to where Mam lies in Grosse Isle, and further still, to Da in Ireland. I wish they were here.

Mam, Da, how can I save Annie? I think, burdened by the lightness of the bag. But I know their answers. They run in my veins.

Pray about it, Mam's words echo in my mind.

You never till a field by turning it over in your mind, Da's advice follows. *Hard work's the way of it.*

And where did that get them? another voice asks.

Only this time, I have no answer.

I face upriver, let the hot breeze take the curls from my sweaty brow. But it doesn't help. 'Tis as though the devil himself is breathing down upon me. Even the boulder beneath me burns like hell's hearthstone. Lord, this July weather is dreadful. Day and night the heat smothers me, and Martha says that August gets even hotter.

My gaze wanders up the river past the falls to the bushy horizon. Jack is up there. Somewhere. Is he finding the adventure he sought? I've had time to think about him, and Mick is right. There's no changing Jack's mind. He's found his adventures. He's living the life he always wanted, even if it kills him. But Mick, poor Mick, he only went because I asked.

How long before he gives up on Jack and comes to Bytown?

Even before the question fully forms, I know the answer.

He isn't coming.

'Twould kill Mick to disappoint me. I know that. If he can't bring me Jack, he won't come to me. His promise to me, his love for me, would be the very thing that would keep him from me.

The pain of it catches my breath, like a stitch in my side, and my pulse pounds in my throat as though I've run a mile to this place of truth. My heart beats against my ribs in anger. It knows, has known all this time. If only my foolish head had listened back home, on the New Ross quay, aboard the *Erin*, or on the shores of Grosse Isle. I suppose I am every bit as stubborn as Jack in my own way. But now, faced with the thought of never seeing Mick again, 'tis finally as clear to me as the cloudless sky.

I've never told Mick how I really feel. Perhaps, I've never really known it myself. How cruel to realize it now. Now that it might be too late.

"Kit!"

I turn to seeing Billy come up the dirt path. "Billy! I hardly recognized you in your new clothes. Look at the state of you, boyo! And a tweed cap, to boot!"

He turns with a flourish, before taking off his cap and bowing to me. "William Farrell, at your service, miss." He smiles that devilish grin of his.

It's great to see him again. I'd seen him in town a few times. Waved in passing but, lugging Mother Bruyere's buckets and baskets, I'd been too busy to stop and chat.

"Where did you get the clothes, Billy? For you didn't nick those from any market stall," I say.

He blushes, remembering that day I got caught. The day he kept on running. But I don't blame him. I would have done the same and I've told him so.

"You are looking at *the* assistant to the assistant of the clerk for one Mr. Sparks." He grins ear to ear.

"Get away!" I shove him in disbelief.

"God's truth, Kit! Oh, you should have seen me. Marched right up to him, so I did, and asked him for an appointment for Mr. William Farrell, Lumber Baron ... and he agrees. Says to tell Mr. Farrell to meet him the next afternoon at the British Hotel."

"No," I say. "What happened?"

Billy grins. "So, he's there having tea at the British Hotel, sitting at a table with nice white linens and all—"

"Waiting for Mr. Farrell," I add.

He nods. "And my heart is pounding in my chest, so it is. I've waited for weeks to meet this man and now's my chance. Now *he's* waiting to meet *me*. But then I realize, 'tisn't me he's waiting on, really. He's expecting a man, right? And then I know exactly what I'm going to say." Billy's face is aglow as he's telling the story. I can only imagine how he must have looked, walking into that hotel that day in his ragged clothes.

"I marched right up to his table. 'Mr. Sparks, sir,' says I, 'I am a huge admirer of yours. I know all about you, how you came to Upper Canada and made a name for yourself. You are my inspiration.' So he pauses, right? His teacup in midair. And the waiter comes over and offers to have me removed, but Mr. Sparks waves him away. He reaches into his pocket and gives me this." Billy pulls out a shiny silver coin. "And he thanks me for the kind words but tells me he has a very important meeting and that I'll have to leave."

"So what did you say?" I ask, for I can see it all unfolding in my mind's eye.

"I asked him if he was waiting for Mr. William Farrell, Lumber Baron. And he nods. And so I tell him—get this, Kit—I say, 'Well Mr. Sparks, sir, I *am* Mr. William Farrell, Lumber Baron ... at least, I will be ... with your help ... in about fifteen years or so, but for now, you can call me Billy.'"

"No!" I burst out laughing. "So what did he do?"

"He did what you are doing," Billy says. "He starts laughing and doesn't stop until there are tears in his eyes. I almost want to run away, but he rests his hand on my shoulder as he catches his breath. 'Billy-lad,' says he, 'that is the best proposal I've heard all day. If you have half as much spunk when you're twice your size, I've no doubt you'll succeed in any endeavor. With or without my help.' He waves over the waiter and I think he's going to have me thrown out, but instead he says, 'John, Mr. Farrell and I will have the steak pies for lunch.' Next thing I know, there am I having steak pies with Nicholas Sparks in the British Hotel!"

I shake my head in disbelief. "Billy, you amaze me, do you know that?"

"He hired me then and there to run errands for his business."

He flips the shiny coin in his hand.

"That must be your lucky coin," I say. For all he's spent, he still has it.

"No," he says, putting it back in his pocket. "I'm saving this for the day I'm a baron in a fancy hotel and some young lad asks for my help."

I've no doubt in my mind that day will come.

"Besides, Kit," he adds, "there's no such thing as a lucky coin. Don't you know? You make your own luck."

CHAPTER THIRTY-EIGHT

"I didn't know you worked as a maid," Sister Phelan says the next morning. She's looking at me, eyebrow raised like Mam would, sussing out a lie. Given my history of impersonating people, I'm not surprised that even a nun has her doubts about me.

"For Lord Fraser," I continue. "He owned our village and many others nearby. I worked at the Big House for a few years before the famine."

"We've had such a hard time keeping up with the laundry. Are you sure you don't want to—"

I shake my head a little too fervently. My days of washing rags and railings are over. Like Billy says, we make our own luck.

"We could always use help visiting the sick and the poor."
She empties her basket for the girls' morning breakfast. Less and
less is in it these days. "In these past few weeks, you know, half
our sisters have fallen ill with typhus; Father Molloy and poor
Martha are down with it."

Another good reason to stop washing infested rags.

I know she needs my help. Waves of Irish continue to break
on the banks of the canal. More and more orphans appear on the
boarding house doorstep. I don't know where they're going to
put them all.

"The Ladies of Charity have been so good with donations
like these." She gestures at the meager pile on the table. "They
visit the poor and sick, but as the disease spreads, more and more
people stay away for fear of catching it themselves."

I can't say I blame them. Had I the money, Annie and I would
be long gone, too.

Sister Phelan looks at me expectantly. I know what she wants
to hear. But I'm no Lady of Charity.

"Sister Phelan," I say. "The sooner I get real work and real
wages, the sooner I'll be able to get out of here. To start a life for

myself and for Annie." I pause. "Isn't that what Saint Raphael's is all about? Helping me help myself?"

She opens her mouth to speak but changes her mind. Sighing, she pats my hand. "Leave it with me, Kathleen. The Lord will provide."

Surprisingly, Sister Phelan gets me a job the next week working for Mr. Miller, of all people. She said someone referred me to him, though I can't think who. Luckily, he doesn't recognize me from that day outside Mr. Sparks's home. It doesn't take long for me to get into the routine of things. I know how and when he likes his tea or his whiskey. Both of them piping hot with sugar, served at any time of day, for he always has meetings of one sort or another going on.

Tea made and tray in hand, I head to the drawing room. Mr. Miller meets me in the hallway and tells me to go ahead and serve his guest. The man sits with his back to me in a wing chair by the fireplace. I don't bother looking, for he's just another suit, the same as all the others Mr. Miller meets. I'm not even sure what kind of business Mr. Miller runs, to be honest.

"Tea, sir?" I set the tray on the table.

"Well, well," he says, his Irish accent smothered in smugness. "If it isn't Kathleen Byrne."

I know the man before I see him, but it doesn't lessen the shock of laying my eyes on none other than Henry Lynch. There he sits, legs crossed, in a fine dark suit, smoking a cigarette. He's found me after all.

I glance at the door.

"Don't bother running." He takes a long drag, reddening the tip, turning it to ash. "I already know where you live. Saint Raphael House, isn't it? The home for wayward girls?" I swallow, but my dry throat snags.

He flicks ash onto the carpet, heedless of where it lands. "Funny," he continues. "I never thought of you as a magdalene. Still ..."

His eyes sweep up my body in a way that makes me blush. Cigarette smoke halos his red hair, slicked back with wax. He's like the devil himself, sitting there in his dark suit with firelight flickering in his eyes.

"I'm not going back to Wicklow Jail," I say, my voice barely a whisper. "I don't care about your inheritance."

He laughs. "So Tom told you, did he? Well, you needn't worry about going back to jail, Kathleen."

I frown, unsure of what he's saying.

Am I free? Is he letting me go?

"Only two things will guarantee I get what's coming to me," he explains. "One, I turn you in myself and claim the bounty. And there's no way I'm crossing that ocean to go back to Ireland. Or two, I make sure *no one else* turns you in and claims the bounty. That would cost me my entire inheritance, and I can't have that." He smiles. "So, you see, I really have no choice." He stands and walks toward me.

I back up against the table, making the teacups rattle in their saucers. My heart pounds in my throat as he slowly approaches, but I'm frozen on the spot like a mouse between cat's paws. I want to scream and run, but I stand and watch him come, step by step, until his jacket presses against my apron and I can smell nothing but the stale smoke on his breath. His eyes hold mine. I cannot even look away. Then with a tiny smile, he reaches past me for a pastry.

"You know," he says, biting into it as he leans over. His crumbs rain upon me. "I never knew what Tom saw in you. But I'm guessing there's more to you than meets the eye." He brushes a crumb off my chest with his finger. "Much more."

I swat his hand away, more from instinct than courage.

"I've been watching you, and you're a survivor, Kathleen, just like me," he says, looking into my eyes.

"I'm nothing like you!"

"No?" He grins and tilts his head. "Tell me. Did you forgive Tom for burning your house?"

I open my mouth to explain, but I have no words.

He laughs but there's no joy in it. "You just left him to die on Grosse Isle, didn't you? We both did. We abandoned Tom to save ourselves." He bites into the pastry again. "We're not so different."

That can't be true. It can't be. But my sinking stomach tells me it is.

"We'll make a pact." He takes my hand in his. "You will work for me and I'll pay you well. Bring me Miller's files."

"You want me to steal?" I say, trying to yank my hand away,

but the vice of fingers closes tight.

"Come, now." His smile is like a daddy-longlegs on my skin. "Who better than a Wicklow Jail inmate like yourself?" He pauses. "I wonder if Mr. Miller knows he's hired a thief, a dirty criminal. Did you tell him you're wanted for trying to kill your previous employer?" His logic closes about me, draws me to his will like a fishnet. No matter how my mind wriggles and flips, there's no breaking free of him.

"And if I say no," I whisper, "you'll tell Mr. Miller about me. I'll lose my job."

"Foolish girl. Who do you think got you this job? Sister Phelan?" He sneers. "I own you. Your job, your life are mine to offer … or to end." He squeezes my hand, and my fingertips throb in time with my racing heart.

My thoughts scurry to find a way out. "All this time," I say with false courage, "you've been watching me. You could have had me arrested."

"Or murdered." He doesn't blink. I know he means it.

"B-but you didn't," I say, as the realization hits me. "You didn't."

Something shifts in his eyes.

He needs me. As long as he needs my help, I'm safe. My job is safe.

"I'll pay you double Miller's wage," he offers.

With twice the money, Annie and I will be free of them all even sooner.

"Deal?" he says, as though he reads my mind.

I swallow and nod as my aching fingers grasp his hand in return.

A pact with Henry Lynch. I'm in league with the devil, but what choice have I?

CHAPTER THIRTY-NINE

I sit on a wooden chair on the other side of Mother Bruyere's desk and wait. Sister Phelan said Mother Bruyere needed to speak to me about something important. I wonder if it is about Mr. Miller.

Her desk is a mess of letters. God knows when she finds the time to write to all those officials, to do all the business of running the hospital, convent, and orphanage. The drippy stub in the candleholder on the edge of the table tells me she must work well into the night.

The spread of typhus is an epidemic now. Immigrants, Bytowners, priests, nuns, hundreds have it. Many have died. Officials shut down the canal at the start of August. No one is allowed in or out, for word has it that typhus has spread from Grosse Isle to towns all along the Saint Lawrence. Sister Phelan tells me that the long-awaited statue of St. Joseph has finally arrived, and the whole congregation is gathering at Notre Dame Cathedral for the novena. They meet every day to pray for St. Joseph's intercession. As if prayers will make any difference. She invited me to join them yesterday. I told her I had to work. What I didn't tell her, is for whom.

I've been meeting Henry Lynch under Sappers Bridge each day for the last few weeks to give him the papers I find on Mr. Miller's desk. I can't read, so I've no idea what he finds so exciting about them, but whatever is in the letters and ledgers seems to make him happy. He's paying me well. I've doubled my wages now. I tell myself 'tisn't stealing, not really, for after Henry reads them, I sneak them back into Mr. Miller's office. What harm is there in that? Come winter, I'll be able to take Annie out of here and this will all be over.

"Ah, Kathleen," Mother Bruyere says, entering the room and sitting across from me. "Thank you for coming. I have something important to discuss with you."

I shift on the hard seat.

She knows. Miller has found out.

"It's about your sister, Annie."

Annie?

She sits and puts on her glasses. Shifting the letters, she finds what she's looking for and reads it over. "The Chartrands live on a big farm near Richmond. They have three little girls, Melanie, Natalie, and petite Valerie. I've met Monsieur Chartrand. He is a good man."

What is she talking about?

"I'm sorry, Mother, but I don't know the Chartrands. Is this about a new job?" There is no way I'd leave Annie to go and work on a farm. Besides, there is no money in that.

She takes off her glasses and looks at me. "*Ma chère*, the Chartrands, they want to adopt Annie."

I laugh at first. But Mother Bruyere's serious expression sobers me.

"There must be some mistake," I argue. "Annie does not need to be adopted. She has me. *I'm* her family."

"You are her sister, Kathleen. She needs a mother and father. The Chartrands, they are—"

"They are *NOT* her family!" I blurt, bolting to my feet. "She's not a Chartrand. She's a Byrne."

"She will keep her last name," Mother Bruyere says. She begins to explain how many orphans keep their Irish surnames. But I still can't get my mind around what she's asking of me. She can't be serious. This isn't happening. There's no way I'm letting them take Annie. She's mine.

"I've been saving my money," I say, "every penny. I'll even show you. I can take care of Annie, Mother. I can." The room feels small all of a sudden. I'm finding it hard to breathe.

"Well, that is the other matter I need to discuss. Mr. Miller has let you go."

"What?" Panic ripples through me and I sit back down. Does he know I've been stealing his papers? If he told on me, I'd surely be kicked out of Saint Raphael's or maybe even sent to Perth Jail. I'd never be able to support Annie then.

"He's gone bankrupt," she says. "Lost it all on a bad deal; the lumber business, the house, everything." Mother Bruyere comes around the desk and stands before me. "I'm sorry, Kathleen. I know you enjoyed working there. Perhaps I can ask the new owner if he would need your services." She lifts another letter, adjusts her glasses. "His name is Lynch, Henry Lynch."

My God, what have I done?

"But even with a job, *ma chère*, you could not give Annie what she needs. It takes more than money to raise a child."

"I can do it!" I say. "I've gotten her to speak again, haven't I?" She doesn't say much, but still … "She needs me. Please, Mother. Give me a chance."

She tucks her hands inside her sleeves. "I have prayed on it much. Letting the Chartrands adopt Annie gives you both a better chance. They are coming for her this Saturday. You must trust God's will, Kathleen."

My head pounds as the thoughts boil inside. "But I love her. The Chartrands, they don't even know Annie."

"Anyone who knows Annie loves her. And if you truly love her, Kathleen, you will want what's best for her," she says gently, resting her hand on my shoulder. "You will let her go *because* you love her."

"No!" I shout, pushing her hand away and breaking free from the tiny room. "I'll never let her go. Do you hear me? Never!"

CHAPTER FORTY

I find Annie feeding the chickens in the yard behind the boarding house. When Martha goes back inside to fetch something, I wave Annie over, careful to stay hidden by the bushes. Surely Mother Bruyere suspects my plans. I've no time to waste.

"Annie, would you like to come with me on an adventure?" I ask. "We can't tell anyone, though. 'Tis our secret."

She looks over her shoulder.

"It's a treasure hunt," I add.

A smile flickers in her eyes and she nods.

We cross the street in front of the cathedral and climb the bluff. Stopping at the flat stone near the edge, I lift it and tell

Annie to look underneath. She picks up the bag and shakes it, her eyes lighting up at the sound of the coins.

"Kit!" she whispers. "We're rich!"

Far from it, I'd say, for surely we'd only enough in there to last us a week or two. But I have other plans. I grab her hand and we run up Sussex for Upper Town. The coins jangle in the bag swinging from her fist, tempting her with their promise of lemon drops and candy sticks. She tries to slow as we pass Sparrow's General Store but I yank her onward.

"The thing about treasure, Annie, is that someone's always trying to take it from you."

"Pirates in Bytown?" She looks over her shoulder, eyes wide. But her pace quickens just the same.

We stop at Miller's house. Or Lynch's, I should say. Using my servant's key, I let myself in.

"Ah, Kathleen." Lynch sits at the table fiddling with a deck of cards. He splits it and grabs half in each hand. "Just in time to make me my tea."

"I need money," I say.

"You and every other Irish farmer fresh off the boat," he

replies, as he fans the cards' top edges together. He bends the halves until they look like the arch under Sappers Bridge. Our meeting place. Then, lowering his finger, he forces the cards to slap and slip one atop the other into one pile again. Annie is mesmerized by it, but I won't be fooled by his tricks.

"You owe me, Henry," I say, stepping forward.

"I owe you nothing," he says, meeting my eyes. Demands won't work with him; I should know that. My only trump card is the fact that if someone else arrests me, he'd lose his inheritance.

"Give me some money and I'll disappear. I've done it before; I can do it again. I'll take a new name. Kathleen Byrne will be as good as dead." I cringe as the words leave my lips, for the last thing I want is to remind him of his other option—to kill me.

"You'd sell out your family name for a few coins?" he says with a smirk. He cascades the cards from one hand to the other, but his eyes never leave mine.

I nod vigorously. "I will. I swear. No one will find me. The bounty money will never get paid. Your inheritance will be yours.".

He looks at me with admiration. For a moment, I think he's going to agree.

"You're right about the inheritance," he says as he leans back in his chair. "In fact, I already have it. Oh, did you not hear?" He clasps his hands behind his head and grins. "My father died last month."

"What?!" The news stuns me. I can't believe it. "All this time, you let me think the bounty was still on my head."

"What sort of a card player tips their hand?" he asks. "If you'd done the job properly the first time and killed the old man, I would have taken my inheritance and left that Godforsaken country. Instead, I had to hunt you down. But you did prove useful after all. My inheritance gave me something to invest, but knowing Miller's business from the inside out, that gave me the edge. I knew I couldn't lose."

"You are a liar and a thief! You destroyed a man's livelihood!"

"No, Kathleen," he smiles, thoroughly enjoying this conversation. "*You* did. You stole from the very man who paid your wages. If anyone is a deceiver here, it's you."

I cringe at the thought of all I'd given Henry Lynch. Of my role in Miller's downfall. Miller was an upper-class snob, but he didn't deserve this betrayal.

"Look at me," Lynch brags. "Not two months in Bytown and I'm already a lumber baron."

I can't take his smug face any longer. I storm out of the house with Annie in tow. He'll not help me. I don't know why I thought he would. Any fool should know a deal with the devil gets you nothing but burned.

Annie and I hide out on the streets of Bytown for the next two days. I try to make it exciting for her, try to keep the panic from my eyes as we eat our meager meals in alleyways and sleep in empty boats. We've enough coins to feed us for a week or two, if that. But I've no job and no plan. I'd thought of looking for Joe Murphy, but if the Chartrands live in Richmond, 'tis the last place I'm taking Annie.

"Kit?" Annie says as we settle in for the third night in our rowboat banked along the canal. She leans back against me looking up at the stars. Without Tish at her side speaking for her, Annie's talking more. Becoming her old self again. "When are we going home?"

"Ireland is very far away, pet," I explain.

"Not Ireland," she says. "The boarding house."

"That's not your home, Annie," I say. It pains me to think she sees it like that.

"Mother Bruyere said I'm getting a real home soon." She turns to face me, her eyes wide in the moon's light. She seems excited. "And three new sisters and a new mammy and—"

"She told me," I say; I don't want to hear it again. I take her small hands in mine. "But don't you want me to be your mammy? I'll take care of you."

Annie frowns as she glances around, and then smiles, like I'm pulling her leg. "No, a *real* mammy. Not one that runs from pirates and digs treasure. Not one that sleeps in old boats."

She lies back on me and her breathing deepens; soon enough she's sound asleep.

What does she know? I tell the stars. *She's only a child.*

We won't be sleeping in boats. We won't be on the run. Not if I can help it. All I need is more money.

The cathedral bell tolls in the distance.

And I know just where to find it.

CHAPTER FORTY-ONE

We're up with the dawn, as stiff as the old boards we slept upon. But it doesn't matter. We won't be sleeping like this again, for I've a plan now.

The roads are near empty for a Saturday morning. Only a few farmers are on their way to the market. Thankfully, we don't see a soul the whole way down Sussex to the steps of Notre Dame Cathedral. Just as I'd hoped, there is no one around to see us slip inside the great stone church. Father Molloy is sick with typhus. The sisters are at morning prayers in their tiny chapel behind the convent, praying for miracles. But I'm going to make a miracle of my own.

The red candle burning next to the tabernacle and the choir of flames before Our Lady are just enough light for the work at hand. Sticking to the shadows, I pull Annie to the far right and up to the front. There it is, hanging on the side wall. Small, black, and metal: the Poor Box.

Letting go of Annie's hand, I try my servant's key in the lock. Sure enough, after a bit of fiddling, it opens and I set the lid on the ground. 'Tis full, for the novena had brought parishioners to the church in droves. I grab a handful. Red candlelight glints off the coins, cold and heavy in my sweating palms. Three months wages, just like that.

I'm not stealing, not really. The money is meant for the poor, meant to help the needy. And I've never felt more in need than I do now.

Annie kneels at the altar rail, her back to me, but the jingle of coins catches her attention and she comes over. "Can I have one?" she whispers.

I almost don't want to give it to her. Don't want the sin of it on her shoulders. For, truth be told, I am stealing from the Church.

From God himself.

The thought chills me. But before I can say no, she reaches up and takes one from my shaking hands.

We're damned now, the both of us.

But Annie doesn't drop it in her pocket like I thought she would. Instead, she reaches past me and slips the penny inside the slit at the front of the Poor Box. It clinks against the others still inside. Taking my other hand, she leads me to the altar rail where she scans the rows of identical tiny cups, searching for the candle that is hers.

She lights the narrow stick from another candle and passes the flame to her own. Then, snuffing the stick, she clasps her hands together and kneels before Our Lady. The candlelight catches the gold in Annie's hair, shining like a halo around her bowed head. "Thank you for my new family," she whispers. "Bless Kit when I'm gone, for she'll have no one but you to look after her."

I swallow the lump in my throat and raise my eyes to the statue. In all the times I'd been in here cleaning dirty corners, I'd never really looked up. My eyes take in the hissing snake's head beneath Mary's bare feet, her blue mantle trimmed in gold, her pristine white dress. It looks so real. Like folds of soft cotton, not cold, chiseled marble. Her upturned hands reach from under her mantle as though waiting for me to hand her something. Squeezing my fist of heavy coins, I push my gaze to her face, knowing what I'll see there. I've imagined it on Mam's face a million times these past few months. I deserve it.

Judgment. Blame. Disappointment.

But instead, in the flickering light, I see something else. Perhaps my eyes are playing tricks, but it almost looks like ... understanding.

All this time, I told myself I was doing what my parents would have wanted. I did whatever it took to keep the family together. I glance down at the coins in my sweaty fist.

Mam would never have wanted this.

I know what Mam and Da would have wanted. What Annie wants. To have a real family again. To have a chance at happiness. I can't deny her that. All I can offer Annie is a life on the streets, a life of thieving and running.

I step back to the Poor Box and drop the coins inside, but it doesn't lighten my burden as I kneel beside my Annie one last time.

"... and send me a puppy. Amen." She finishes, blessing herself.

One tear rolls along my nose and drops into her hair as I kiss the top of her head, for I know now what I have to do.

I only wish I wanted to do it.

The Chartrands' wagon waits outside the boarding house when we leave the cathedral. Mother Bruyere sees us coming down the street and acts like we'd just been out for a morning stroll.

"Kathleen, Annie," she says, resting her hand on my shoulder for reassurance, or perhaps to hold me there. "This is Monsieur and Madame Chartrand."

They seem nice enough. Hard-working people. Salt of the earth, Mam would say.

"Are you my new Mammy?" Annie asks the woman.

Madame Chartrand kneels and places her hand on Annie's chest. "Your mammy is in heaven and in your heart. But if you like, I will be your *Maman*."

"And you can call me *Papa*," Monsieur Chartrand adds.

Annie slips her hand into Madame Chartrand's. She smiles at Mother Bruyere. "I'll take them."

They laugh. But I don't.

I can't do this. I can't say goodbye to my Annie.

As if reading my thoughts, Mother Bruyere takes my hand and squeezes it.

"I'm 'dopted, too!" Tish calls from the wagon and Annie runs to her.

Letting go of Mother Bruyere's hand, I walk to Annie and lift her up to the wagon.

"Bye, Kit," she says, hugging me tight.

I can't speak. Can't breathe. My words are smothered in pain. I lived to find her, to keep her. What will I live for now?

Annie pulls away and settles herself beside Tish. Seeing them together helps. They still have each other. For all the hours I'd been working *for* Annie, I have to admit, I'd really spent very little *with* her. She won't miss me. Not like I'll miss her.

The Chartrands say goodbye to Mother Bruyere and invite me to visit anytime. But how can I? How can I see Annie in a family that isn't my own?

Mr. Chartrand snaps the reins.

"Kit!" Annie clutches the wagon's sideboards and waves the bag of remaining coins overhead. "Your treasure!"

If she only knew what treasure that wagon truly holds.

"Buy your puppy with it!" I call, as they roll away. Her face breaks into a huge smile, filling her cheeks and igniting her eyes, making her look almost like her old self. No amount of money will ever buy my dreams. I see that now.

The least they can do is buy Annie's.

CHAPTER FORTY-TWO

The days roll into each other. What does it matter? I have no job, but what need have I of money? Mam and Da are gone. Jack and Mick, and now my Annie, all lost. I have nothing. I feel nothing. I am nothing, for I'm neither daughter nor sister anymore. I've neither purpose for today, nor hope for tomorrow. And even though I've willed myself a thousand times to sleep and never wake again, even though I curse the sun that rises, still the morning comes.

Day after day after day.

Mother Bruyere sends for me from her sick bed. So wrapped up in my own misery I didn't even know she was ill, has been for nearly two weeks. I enter the tiny room in the convent house to find her lying in bed, pale-faced and drawn. Her white-capped head turns as I enter and she smiles weakly. She whispers something in French to Sister Thibodeau sitting on the one chair in the room and Sister Thibodeau leaves us alone.

"How are you faring, Mother Bruyere?" I ask, for she doesn't look well.

"I was about to ask you the same thing." She motions for me to sit on the chair beside her. "Sister Phelan tells me you are not working or eating."

I nod.

"That makes two of us. Such a waste, *non*?"

I don't answer.

"There is so much to be done and yet, here we are. I suppose the least we can do is pray for their work. Will you pray with me, *chère*?" She lifts her rosary from the side table, blesses herself, and begins, but when she pauses for my response, the words don't come.

"A Bible story, then?" she says, taking her black book from

the table. It reminds me of Mam's old Bible. "Perhaps learning the stories will help you—"

"I don't need to learn them," I blurt. "I *lived* them!"

The outburst catches us both by surprise and I apologize for it.

"Mother," I continue, "I've lived through famine. I've sailed for forty days and nights. Swallowed by a whale or a ship's hull, isn't it one and the same? Aren't I exiled from my promised land?" My voice catches and I stop to breathe. "I'm living the life of Job, Mother. One tragedy after another."

We sit in silence for a few minutes.

"Do you believe in God, Kathleen?" she finally asks. Her question catches me by surprise. No one ever asked me that before. In all the years of people telling me what to believe, no one ever asked me if I did. I'd never dared to ask it of myself.

Do I?

I hold the question, consider its weight, before tossing it like a wishing coin and watching it sink in the deepest, darkest part of me.

Do I?

... do I?

Yes.

The answer surprises me as it surfaces and ripples through me. But I know it to be true.

"I believe … but I do not understand. Why did all this have to happen? Where was God in all this?"

She reaches for my hand. "Kit, great faith lives beside great doubt. If we had all the answers, we would not need faith. Look at me. Two and a half years ago, I was sent to a town known for its wildness and riots. Do you think it was easy? Do you think I wasn't scared? But I trusted God, and look at all he has done here."

She's right. I can only imagine where all those immigrants would be if she hadn't been here to help them. To help Annie. To help me.

"But you are Mother Bruyere," I say. "I'm an orphan; I have nothing. I am nothing."

"In here," she points to her chest, "I am Élisabeth. I, too, am an orphan. I grew up in poverty. I saw my father die. I have fears and doubts. I miss my home and my family in Montreal." Her eyes well. "I still struggle with that. I feel what you feel, Kathleen."

I didn't realize. She always seems so sure. "But you have your work and your sisters. You have hope," I add.

She nods and squeezes my hand. "You had hope, too. But you put it in the wrong things. In people and places. In money. In all you could achieve by will or work. Those things will always let you down. You know that to be true, now. Try putting your hope in God. God alone."

She knows. Someone truly knows how I feel, how it has been for me. It doesn't change anything, yet somehow everything is different, as though someone lit a small sputtering candle in my darkness.

I wipe my nose with the back of my hand and rest my head on the side of her bed. "I used to be a daughter and a sister. For a while, I was even a boy. But I am none of those now. I'm lost, Mother. I don't even know who I am anymore."

"I do, *chère*." She rests her hand on my head. "You are Kathleen Byrne."

CHAPTER FORTY-THREE

"I figured you'd be here," Martha says, joining me at the top of the bluff where I sit and stare out at the black river.

"Sister Phelan will have a conniption if she sees you sitting in that," I mumble, as she settles beside me in her new brown robe and sets the basket beside her. She'd traded her purple dress for the nun's habit after taking her novice promises a few days ago.

"I'm still not used to you looking like that," I add. She looks like a nun, save for the silver cross and ring she'll get when she takes her final vows after her training in Montreal. But I have to admit, she's glowing like a new bride.

"The coach for Montreal leaves in a few hours." She offers

me an apple but I shake my head. "I just wanted to say goodbye."

I pick up a curled, brown leaf and twiddle it in my fingers. "So you're leaving me, too."

But she doesn't answer.

"I love the start of fall," she says, cracking into her apple, slurping its juice. "The apples. The geese getting ready to fly. The blushing maples." She breathes deeply, drawing it all inside of her.

I see only loss and leaving. A cold, dark winter ahead. All of it mourned with waning honks. The leaf crumbles, leaving dust in my hands.

"So, I suppose I'm a goose now myself," she says, patting her black bonnet and smiling at my surprised expression. "Oh, I know all about Rose's nicknames. So does Sister Phelan. But what better animal could we be, really?"

She waits, making me ask, even though I don't feel like talking.

"What do you mean?" I finally say; she has me curious now.

She points at another wide arrow of birds approaching from the north. "See how they fly together like that, in a v?"

I'd wondered about that.

"My father told me that the wind from each one's flapping wings uplifts the goose behind. By working together, they raise each other up." She squints up at them as they soar over our heads. "And when the leader is tired, another takes a turn."

Just as she says it, the arrow shifts and a new goose takes the lead. The geese fly on, loose and yet linked together, like a string of black beads shrinking into the horizon.

"How is Mother Bruyere?" I ask, afraid of the answer. "Is it typhus?"

Martha shakes her head. "Meningitis. She's in great pain. Doctor Van Cortlandt is with her now." Her answer has no reassurance for either of us. She takes the basket beside her and hands it to me. I'd know that worn handle anywhere; it's Mother Bruyere's. The basket's emptiness makes it feel heavier than ever.

"You are to take over her route while she is ill," Martha says, standing and brushing off her skirts. "She specifically asked for you."

"I can't do it." *All those families? Is she mad?* "I'm not Mother Bruyere. Can't you ask someone else?"

"There is no one else," Martha answers. More and more sisters are in the grip of typhus. More and more volunteers are abandoning the work in fear. Yet, none of it smothers the hopefulness in Martha's voice. "... but there is you."

"Me?" I scoff. "You can't ask me to do what she did."

Martha smiles and hugs me goodbye. She smells like apple. "Do what Kit can do," she says gently as she lets me go. "That's all God asks."

Though I can't collect anywhere near what Mother Bruyere would, it seems the families are glad of whatever I bring that week. Their faces light up when they see me and they're so thankful for the bit of bread or fish I give them, the new blanket, or the hot cup of tea. Such little things, really, and yet, they mean so much.

With so many families to visit, on my first round I don't want to stop and chat. I've enough to do without having to listen to all that. But it doesn't take me long to realize there's no stopping an Irishman with a tale to tell. Truth be told, there's no rushing them neither. So I stand there, hand on the door, shifting foot to foot while Widow Moore goes on and on about her bad hip, or while

Meg tells me about her baby's dry nappies, or while Frankie Brady natters on about the "big one that got away" that afternoon as he fished in the river with a branch and a bit of twine.

Funnily enough, listening makes my work easier. For every story makes me a better beggar. I'll rap that Upper Town brass doorknocker and ask for milk for Meg's baby who needs a sup, or a blanket for Widow Moore whose old joints ache in the damp nights, or some fish for Frankie Brady to replace the one that got away. I'll do it and do it boldly, for I know if I don't, they'll go without. For the most part, Bytowners are generous. When they hear the stories of need, when I ask for something specific, almost always they offer it.

All this time, I thought they didn't care, but maybe, just maybe, they didn't understand.

Each day that week, I end my visits at the Bradys' home so I can help Theresa. As always, Frankie sits on the boarding house steps waiting for me and runs to carry my basket the last bit of the way. By then, my arms are like two lead logs swinging from my shoulders. He's sporting a black eye today, but only shrugs when I ask where he got it. Fortunately, Agnes's fever has broken. I wash her face and arms, comb her hair, and change her clothing, like I've seen Mother Bruyere do. Taking off her dirty shift, I toss it with my laundry pile and then slip a fresh one gently over her head. She takes a drink and a small bit of bread, a bite more than yesterday.

"Rest," I tell her. "The worst of it's over now."

She smiles weakly as I lay her back down. Cups in hand, the children gather round me as their mother sleeps.

"Can I tell my one about the Wild Geese?" Frankie asks.

Theresa scolds him for bringing it up. She remembers how it upset me last time.

I sigh; he's relentless, that one. Just like Jack. "Go on, then."

"'Twas many years ago," he starts, lisping his gap-toothed way through the well-told tale. "When thousands of Irish left." He hesitates. "Because they couldn't get treats from Limerick."

"You mean because of the Treaty of Limerick," I say.

"Right," Frankie nods. "And so they all climbed into a boat."

"All twenty-four thousand of them?" I ask.

"Uh-huh. The boats were much bigger then," he explains.

Theresa *tsks* at his foolishness.

"... and they sailed," Frankie scrunches up his face, "they sailed for forty days and nights aboard the *Perseverence* until they reached a land of milk and honey." He holds up his bowl. "And stew."

"*Perseverence*?" Theresa interrupts. "Don't be silly, Frankie. That's the ship we came on."

"'Tis my story, Theresa," he snaps. "This is the way it goes. And the Wild Geese landed in the foreign land. They had many great epic battles for survival. Especially the one against Timmy Duncan."

"Timmy Duncan?" Theresa blurts. "Timmy Duncan from down the lane? You're making that up," she scoffs and turns to me. "Is that how it goes, Kit?"

I glance at Frankie and shake my head. "Sorry, Frankie. I don't recall the part about Timmy Duncan."

"See?" Theresa says. "That's not the real story at all."

Frankie bolts to his feet, spilling what little stew he had. His hands are clenched by his side and his watery eyes glare at the pair of us. "It *is* a real story, Theresa. It is! It's *MY* story. I fought Timmy Duncan this very day down by the canal. He tried to take my firewood. But I wouldn't let him, so he threw me on the ground and gave me this." He points at his shiner. "We fought for five whole minutes, Theresa. And I won! I *WON*! I got the firewood to heat Mam's stew so she can get better." His tiny body shakes with emotion.

He knows neither the Irish Jacobites of the 1690s, nor the soldiers from the wars fought many years after. Frankie Brady knows only the battles he fights every day in this new land a long, long way from home. Battles for firewood and food. Battles for survival. His Wild Geese story.

"Five whole minutes?" I say, taking his tiny fist in my hand. "Why, Frankie Brady, that surely is an epic battle if ever I heard one."

His hand opens in mine and I pull him into my lap. I can feel his tiny heart throbbing in his bony chest. He takes a few deep breaths and lets the tension go out of him, like a rope gone slack.

"Will you tell me yours, Kit?" Frankie says, staring into the embers glowing in the tiny fire pit. "Will you tell me your Wild Geese story?"

And tell it I do.

CHAPTER FORTY-FOUR

After a few weeks and many prayers, Mother Bruyere recovers. The sisters say 'tis a miracle. Even Dr. Van Cortlandt seems surprised by her healing. Of the fifteen sisters that caught typhus, not one of them died, which is a miracle in itself, given the number of Bytowners it claimed.

When Mother Bruyere returns to her rounds, I offer to carry her baskets. She smiles and thanks me, though, in all honesty, I should be thanking her. I want to see the face of Mr. Doolen when I give him back his patched shirt, or Sarah Meehan's when I hand her a few shiny apples. I need to see them. Besides, Widow Moore is teaching me how to crochet a blanket for Meg's baby, and Frankie has only heard a tenth of my stories yet. God only knows how many of his he's yet to tell.

Mother Bruyere is amazed at how much I've thrown myself into the duties she'd left me. She well knows how little I wanted them, and even more so, how badly I needed them. So, week after week, Mother Bruyere and I beg for donations from market stalls, butchers, and bakers. Even Mr. Desjardins generously hands me three loaves, though I doubt he recognizes me. Still, it feels redeeming to hear him wish me well and praise the work. Daily we cross Sappers Bridge and ask the citizens to share what they have, building little bridges between poor and rich, Irish and French, Protestant and Catholic, one loaf of bread, one pot of soup at a time.

Mother Bruyere and I pass Sparrow's General Store on our way home one evening. 'Tis bitter cold and near dark as we cross the street, carefully navigating the ruts of frozen mud. Shorter days just mean we have to work faster, for there isn't less need in winter. If anything, there's more. I've been knitting well into the night at Saint Raphael's but, even then, I can't work fast enough to meet the demands. Ready or not, winter is coming.

"I wonder if Mr. Sparrow would donate a few sets of needles and balls of wool," I say, as the idea drifts into my mind like a snowflake from the darkness. "I could teach the children how to knit. Why, we could knit enough socks for every bare foot in Bytown!"

Mother Bruyere smiles. "You make your mother proud."

Her words pause in the cold air for a second before disappearing into the night. I don't know if she meant Mam, or Our Lady, or even herself, but a blacksmith's bellows could not have fired up the warmth those few words gave me.

Rose tells me about Canadian winters, but surely she's exaggerating. They can't be as long, or deep, or brutal as she says. Can they? I'd seen snow before; hadn't we had some in Ireland from time to time? A light sprinkling, like God had sifted a bit of flour over the land. When the winter starts, truly starts, and the heavens open upon us, I realize Canadian snow is a dumping, not a dusting. Rose isn't joking. Some days it falls for hours, blanketing the world in great downy flakes. Other days it shoots across the frozen river, pricking our cheeks with its ice needles. But whatever the weather, we bundle up and do our rounds. Our friends are waiting.

As the winter wears on, I teach the children we visit and the girls in the orphanage how to knit. Mr. Sparrow and the Ladies of Charity donate the wool; some are the colors no one would buy, and others are leftover bits from their knitting, but the girls are glad to have it. Their cold little fingers work the sloppy stitches, in-around-through, in-around-through, just as I've taught them. 'Tis slow going, to be sure. Painfully slow and, truth be told, with all their dropped stitches, there's more hole than sock. After a few weeks, most have only a multi-colored mess to show for all their efforts. Even Theresa Brady, my prize student, has only finished the one sock. Frankie wears it on his right foot, proudly shows it to us when we get there. But I feel discouraged. At this rate, winter will be over before they finish their knitting, and what good is that?

Mother Bruyere reminds me that one sock is warmer than none and that I've given them something more than a bit of clothing. I've given them a purpose and taught them the skill to do it. By next winter, she says, the children will have finished two pairs each. I wish I had her patience and her vision.

For, try as I might, all I can think about is Frankie's cold left foot.

CHAPTER FORTY-FIVE

"What do you think you're doing?" Rose asks one night by the fire at Saint Raphael's. All the other girls are long asleep.

I hold up the knitting needles. "Isn't it obvious?"

"Not that," she scoffs, "with them. The sisters. You waste all your time with them."

'Tis true. My days revolve around the sisters' schedules— getting food; delivering it to the sick and poor; I even follow their prayer times. At first, my prayers are dry and empty. But when I think of the families, of all they need, the words spill out of me. I pray for Theresa and Frankie, for Agnes, for Widow Moore, for the sisters; I light candles for Jack and Annie, for Lizzie, for

Mick. Even for Rose.

"And didn't I see you go in the confessional last week?" she says, like she's asking if it was me she saw jumping off Sappers Bridge.

I stop knitting and look at her. I hadn't realized she'd seen me that day. To be honest, I hadn't planned on going. One minute I was polishing the kneeler by the confessional, the scratched one Mr. Fitzgibbon refinished, and the next thing I knew I was on my knees in the confessional, baring every shameful secret I'd ever carried.

I'd that dusting rag twisted in knots in my sweaty hands as I told Father Molloy how I'd tried to poison Lynch, how I'd let Tom die unforgiven, how I'd stolen Miller's livelihood. It all rushed out of me, my sins of murder, envy, hatred, theft, deceit, doubt, anger, and greed. It sickened me to bring them up and spew them out—but I had to. I just had to. For I could carry them no longer.

"Yes," I admit to Rose, as though confessing my sins were more shameful than committing them. "In truth, I half expected Father Molloy to whip open the door, drag me by the scruff of my neck, and toss me down the cathedral steps."

Her eyes widen as if seeing me for the first time. She leans forward. "B'Jaysus, Kit, I'd like to hear what you told him."

"I can't tell you that," says I, going back to my knitting. "But I can tell you what he said. Three little words I'll never forget." I pause and look at her hanging on to my every word. "You. Are. Forgiven."

She catches herself sitting on the edge of her chair and rolls her eyes as she flops back. "As if." She folds her arms and frowns at the fire. I wonder what she's thinking. "Like I want Father Molloy bellowing fire and brimstone at me," she mutters. "No thanks. I don't need his forgiveness."

"'Tisn't his you're asking for," I say, avoiding her glare.

"What do you know, anyway?" she stands and spits the words at me. "Carrying a nun's basket doesn't make you holy, Kit. Sure, any old ass could do that. So don't go getting all high and mighty with me."

I have to laugh, for she's right. But my laughter only makes her scowl all the more. She stomps up the stairs to our room. I knit for a little while longer as the fire dies.

I like carrying the baskets and helping the families in need. I like working with the sisters. What's wrong with that? In these past few months, Mother Bruyere has taught me so much. She has given me a sense of purpose. A belief in God. A belief in myself. She has taken me from the muddy streets of Bytown and patiently helped me knit my life together, holes and all, just like Frankie's sock.

"How did you know you were meant to be a nun?" I ask Sister Phelan, as we trudge through the drifts on our way to the market the next morning. She smiles to herself as though my question isn't unexpected, though surely 'tis to me. "Did an angel appear to you or a vision or something?"

Her laughter comes out in puffs of steam. "No, nothing like that. For me, it was just a knowing. A sense of coming home. Like I belonged."

We walk in silence, listening to our boots crunching the fresh snow. I want to belong, more than anything. Only I don't know for sure where that is.

"Nobody knows right away, Kathleen," she explains. "At least, nobody I've met. We all had to discern, you know, spend time learning and thinking and praying about our path."

I nod. It makes sense, really. "Can you show me how to discern?"

She smiles. "Step one: become a postulant."

A *postulant*?

The word catches me by surprise and I don't say anything more the rest of the way. But the more I think about it, the more it makes sense. 'Tis no different really than my days now, for I'd be working with the sisters, praying with them, learning from them. I talk to Mother Bruyere about it when we get back from the market, and she is even less surprised by my interest than Sister Phelan was.

"Becoming a Sister of Charity means taking vows of poverty ..."

I've no penny to my name

"... obedience ..."

I want you to tell me what to do ...

"... dedication to serving the poor ..."

I spend my days doing that already ...

"... and chastity."

I hesitate at this one. I'd always assumed I'd have children of my own one day. A family.

Am I really willing to give all that up?

"Do not worry about having the answers now," she says. "A postulant is meant to question and search. After a year, you will know if this is your path or not. Then you will decide. Today, you need only decide if you want to know more."

"Yes, Mother," I say wholeheartedly. "I do."

Two weeks later, I don a purple postulant dress and white bonnet. I take all I own in this world, the black rosary Father Robson gave me, and I leave Saint Raphael's to join the sisters in the convent.

CHAPTER FORTY-SIX

And so the winter wears on. A land of extremes, this Canada, for the same blossoming branches outside our house now hang heavy in their sheaths of ice. Mother Bruyere tells me February is known for its bite. Bite? says I. Cold Irish rain has bite. But this winter hound gnaws me to the bone every time I trudge up Sussex, and no amount of sweaters, mitts, nor muffs can protect me. On those nights when the thick drifts lean upon our frosted windows, it takes me a good hour by the fire before I feel my fingers and toes. I swear that blistering summer heat must be a dream I had.

The wave of typhus has subsided, thank God, but the frigid

winter ensures our hospital beds are always full. My afternoons are spent working with Sister Thibodeau in the house used for a hospital. I am learning so much from her. It reminds me of working with Lizzie back home.

Agnes Brady has recovered, but now her children are consumptive, their tiny bodies wracked with such coughing fits, it sounds like they'll never stop. Widow Moore is well enough to keep complaining, but Meg's baby hadn't the strength for this harsh life. Sadly, it died last month.

We often have a few lumbermen brought to our doorstep, usually suffering from axe wounds or frostbite, for we are the only hospital for miles around. Every time I see one of them, I think of Jack and Mick, wonder if they are alive or dead. For, by the look of these grizzled men, life in the bush is no great adventure, and certainly no life for boys.

I'm surprised to find Billy sleeping in one of the hospital beds when I arrive one afternoon. I haven't seen him in ages. His arm and leg are splinted, he's missing a front tooth, and his head is swaddled in bandages.

"Kit?" he says, waking as I enter with a tray of soup for him and the other four patients in the tiny room. His fat lip splits when he speaks.

"What happened?" I ask.

"I was about to ask you the same thing." He takes in my postulant's dress. "The purple brings out the bags under your eyes."

"Listen to that cheek," I say, as I hand him his bowl. "I should break your other leg for that."

He gasps in mock surprise. "Take a vow of violence, did you? Such hostility for a nun."

"Yes, well, I'm not one yet."

As much as I enjoy working with the sisters, I feel restless, unsettled. I've none of the knowing Sister Phelan described, nor the sense of coming home Martha once mentioned. I talked to Mother Bruyere about it last week, admitted my concerns.

"I don't think I'm meant to be a sister, Mother," I'd said. It felt like a failure to admit it. "I like the work, but the road ahead seems as lost to me as a drift in a snowstorm."

"Do the work before you and trust that your path will show itself," was all she said, her answer as clear as a blizzard.

I look at the three bowls of soup that need handing out. I'll do the work before me. But even I know you can't be a postulant forever. What then?

"Speaking of violence, how did you get yourself into this mess?" I ask, returning to Billy's bedside.

He shrugs. "Wrong place at the wrong time."

"I'd say."

I wait for him to tell the tale but, surprisingly, he doesn't.

"Still working for Mr. Sparks?" I ask. "I'd have thought you'd be Lord Mayor by now."

He looks into his soup but doesn't lift his spoon. "Remember what I said about making your own luck, Kit?"

I nod, thinking of the day he appeared on the bluff in his fine new clothes. I wonder where they went, considering the rags he now wears.

"'Tisn't true. Not really. You can make all the luck you like. The thing is, there's always someone bigger, someone luckier who can take it away from you."

Right after Annie left, I would have agreed with him. I thought of all that was taken from me this long year and, for the first time, realized all I'd gained. I'd found faith, hope; I'd found my *Anam Mór*, as Murph had called it all those long months back in the belly of that ship. Great Soul. Now, I finally understood.

"No matter what they take from you," I sit on the bed and rest my hand on Billy's heart as Murph's words echo through me, "they can't take what's in here. And with that, why, you've got all you need."

His clenched lips don't stop his chin from quivering. I can't tell if it's from his broken hope or his broken bones. Either way, I'll leave him be. Standing, empty tray in hand, I head to the kitchen, for I've more soup yet to give.

"Kit," he calls, stopping me at the doorway. "Thanks."

I smile. "Eat your soup, now," I say as I go. I know well enough you shouldn't force hope any more than pry open a cocoon. It has to emerge in its own time.

All we can do is wait. And watch for its fluttering.

CHAPTER FORTY-SEVEN

The wagon splashes me in chilly slush as it races past and stops just ahead, outside the hospital. An older lumberman jumps from the driver's seat. His plaid shirt is drenched in red and his bloodied right hand is missing a few fingers. Dropping my basket in the snow bank, I run to help him.

"Your hand! Good Lord! Are you all right?" I try to get him to sit on the running board as I call for Sister Thibodeau, but he won't settle. He must be in shock.

"Non, non … not me!" He clasps my hand firmly with his bloodied thumb and finger. The strength of it surprises me, but as he leads me around to the back of the wagon, I realize his maiming is an old injury. 'Tis not his blood. Another lumberman lies under a wool blanket with a bloodstained shirt wrapped around his head and most of his face. He's not moving. I wonder if he's alive at all, for what skin I can see is slushy gray and his uncovered lips are blue.

Sister Thibodeau rushes out to join us. "What happened, Benoît?"

"The logjam exploded too early," Benoît says, climbing up by the young man's head. "Don't go, I tell him, it's too dangerous … but he won't listen, him—" his voice catches.

She feels for the injured man's pulse. He's soaked to the skin; his body is a mass of cuts and scrapes Wadded, bloodied rags wrap around his head and pile against his side.

"How long was he in the water for?" she asks as she climbs into the back of the wagon and lifts the sodden rags. His side gushes as she inspects the wound and she quickly presses her hand upon it.

"Two, maybe three minutes. I'm not sure."

"Kathleen," she waves me over and pushes my hand over hers against his side. She slips hers out. "You must press down on this. He has already lost a lot of blood."

She doesn't have to tell me. Doesn't the back of the wagon look like a butcher's floor?

"Will he be all right, Sister Thibodeau?" Benoît asks.

"He's been in the frigid water far too long for my liking. We have to get him inside, now." Laying the blanket beside the lad, she nods at Benoît. Gently, they lift the young man onto the blanket and, each taking the corners, carry him inside. A trail of reddened slush follows us from the wagon to the house.

"Keep that pressure on," Sister Thibodeau scolds as they lay him flat on the first empty bed, but the jostling about makes my job near impossible. Blood gushes between my slick fingers, a sure sign his heart still beats. I pray to God it keeps on going.

"I don't think he's breathing anymore," Sister Thibodeau says, quickly lifting the bandage from around his head so she can listen at his mouth. "We're losing him."

But her words are lost in the drumming of my head. It keeps time with the blood throbbing hot against my hand, the life seeping through my fingers, slowing with every pulse. For as she uncovered his face, I saw 'twas not some young lumberman.

'Tis Mick. My Mick.

CHAPTER FORTY-EIGHT

"Oh, no, you're not," I say, kneeling at the head of the bed by Mick's gray and blood-smeared face. "You can't leave me, Mick. I won't let you."

I'd seen Lizzie do this once, saw her breathe life back into Fanny Conroy the day Fanny fell out of her father's boat and drowned. Or so we all thought. Lizzie had leaned over that lifeless body, blown into it, pumped the heart, and brought her back to life.

What sort of magic had Old Lizzie, everyone wondered. To be able to blow a soul back into a body. What witchery? Surely it meant she could suck out a soul just as easily. As if she didn't scare the b'jaysus out of us already. 'Twasn't until I worked with her those last few months that I asked about it. She told me then how they aren't really dead. Not yet, anyways. Snuffing the candle by the bed doesn't mean you're asleep. For those first few moments, you're in that space between awake and dreaming.

Pinching his nose and pulling his chin, I open Mick's mouth, just like Lizzie had done with Fanny that day. I take a deep breath, place my mouth over Mick's icy lips, and blow my will into him. *Wake up! Come on, Mick. Wake up!*

"What are you—" Sister Thibodeau grips my shoulders to pull me away, but Benoît rests his hand on her arm and she stops. I cannot hear her now at any rate, for Lizzie's voice fills my mind.

Blow two breaths, she says, *listen for a whisper.*

I listen, but Mick is still.

Knock thirty times at the heart's crossroads.

Ripping open his sodden shirt, I find where his ribs meet and just as I'd seen Lizzie do, I lock my fingers and plunge down with the heel of my bloodied hands, kneading his heart awake. Needing it awake. Blood spurts from his side with my every push.

Try again.

I blow and knock.

Again.

I blow and knock.

"Kathleen," Sister Thibodeau's voice echoes from afar. "He's gone."

Again! Lizzie says.

How long can you do it for, I'd asked Lizzie that day.

She'd taken a drag of her pipe and thought about the answer. *Well, that depends on which of you's the more stubborn. Who's not letting go? For as long as there's breath in the body, the soul stays. I suppose if you're stubborn enough, you could blow and knock until you were dead yourself. But why would you? If they're ready to go, why keep them here? You well know yourself how it feels to give in to sleep after a long, hard day of it.*

"Don't leave me, Mick, please," I plead, as I plunge his chest.

Lizzie once told me that in that place between awake and dreaming, we often see our loved ones who've gone on before us. They meet us there. As I pump his chest, I look at Mick's eyes, still closed in his bloodied face.

Who waits for him?

His mother.

His father.

His brother, Kenny.

His little sisters, Meg and Nan.

How can I keep him from them? From his family?

After all he's done for me, what right have I to ask anything of him again?

The cold truth of it hits me, numbing the heat of my will. As much as I want him here with me, as badly as I need him to live, I love him too much to make him stay. Moving to his head, I rest my mouth on his one more time, only this time I don't blow. I kiss.

I kiss my Mick goodbye.

CHAPTER FORTY-NINE

"He's breathing!" Sister Thibodeau cries.

I lift my face from the bed where I'd laid it in grief not moments before and rest it on his chest. Sure enough, his heart is beating like a bodhran. He moans and shivers.

"Quickly, we have to get him warm!" Sister Thibodeau orders. Benoît stokes the fire, as Sister Thibodeau strips Mick's wet clothes. I can do nothing but hold my hand against Mick's side. So much blood. His life will surely seep away if we can't stop it. Sister Thibodeau tightly wraps his wounds, but before we can cover him in blankets, deep red seeps through the bandages.

"It isn't stopping," she says. "Kathleen, take Benoît to fetch

Dr. Van Cortlandt."

Moments later, I'm sitting by Benoît, speeding along slushy streets to Upper Town. Neither of us speaks. I can tell by the worry in his eyes, by the way Benoît twisted his cap in his hands while Sister Thibodeau tended to Mick, that he cares for him. But the bushy brows he'd raised in worry are now furrowed in anger. It radiates off him.

"*Hey! Ôtez-vous du ch'min!*" he hollers, and snaps the reigns as Bytowners rush off the road, narrowly avoiding the wagon. "*Maudit batards*," he curses.

Benoît's clenched jaw makes me think twice before asking. Still, I have to know.

"Can you tell me, sir, what happened to Mick?"

He glares at me with such intensity, I'm almost sorry I asked.

"What happened? He was somewhere he should not have been," he says, breaking off in a flurry of French. I don't have to speak the language to know he's cursing a blue streak. "This … *THIS* is what happens when you send someone to do *your* job!"

I cringe under his gaze and look away. So Mick told him. How else would he know I'd sent Mick to watch over Jack?

We stop outside the Van Cortlandt house and collect the doctor. Within minutes, we're racing back to the hospital on St. Patrick Street. Dr. Van Cortlandt rides up front with Benoît while I sit on the red-stained boards in the back. Mick's blood congeals in puddles down the center of the boards. So much blood; yet I can't take my eyes off it.

I should never have forced Mick to go. He's no lumberman.

A crimson puddle creeps toward me as we speed around the corner, but I make no move to avoid it. Benoît is right. This is all my fault. Mick's blood is on my hands.

The doctor works for ages on Mick, stitching him back together while Benoît and I sit vigil in the hall. Benoît hasn't said a word since we returned. He stares at the wall and fiddles with the cap in his hands. Twice now, he's caught me staring at his mangled right hand. I can't help it. 'Tis amazing how deftly he uses what's left, the thumb and finger, like a pair of tongs. I wonder what maiming Mick will have to learn to live with. If he makes it.

"This is all my fault!" I blurt, for I can take Benoît's silence no longer.

He stops fidgeting and looks over at me.

"Mick was in the bush because of me," I say. "I made him go. I should've known better than to ask him." Images flash before my eyes: Mick tripping over his own feet as we run in the fields back home; Mick slipping on the wet rocks and scaring away all the fish; Mick dangling from the yard arm on the *Erin*. "What was I thinking, forcing him into the woods? Mick has always been clumsy. He made a terrible sailor. Surely, he's a worse lumberman."

"*Non*," Benoît shakes his head. "*Non, ma fille*, that Mick, he's no bank beaver, him."

The confusion on my face makes him explain.

"Beavers, they are so hard working, they can't stand any other beaver that is lazy or a misfit. They put him out." He flicks his arm. "And that beaver, he has to live by himself. An easy catch for the trapper, that one. The trappers, they call them bank beavers."

He looks at the door to Mick's room.

"Mick started out helping the cook, cleaning the shanty, whatever odd jobs we gave him. For hours he marked log end after log end with the timber stamp, just so others did not have to. The logs must be stamped with the company brand so other companies don't take them. No one likes that job, especially after their long day's work felling, hauling, and hewing deep in the bush. So Mick, he said he'd do it. And he did. Stamped log after log until he had blisters on his blisters," he shakes his head and smiles. "I said to myself, he has heart, that one. He will make a fine lumberman if someone teaches him."

Benoît pauses and stretches his mangled hand, staring at it as he flips it from side to side, as though seeing it for the first time. "After my accident, Mick took care of me. Sat by me. Made sure my bandages were always clean. I had to learn how to swing the axe and work the two-man saw all over again. And so I taught Mick. He's a fast learner, him. A hard worker." He closes his hand, crosses his arms, and smiles. "Mick, he is my right-hand man."

"But how did he end up in the river?" I ask.

Benoît's eyes grow serious. "Sometimes we get logjams up in the river narrows. Usually the drivers, they use their cant-hooks to break it up. Someone has to climb across the jam to find and free the logs that are causing the blockage. It's so dangerous, the foreman can only ask for volunteers. Over the years, I have buried good friends and great lumbermen who died trying to free the key-logs." He gazes into the floorboards for a moment. When he continues, his voice is hoarse. "I can't volunteer anymore. I've lost my nerve. But it should have been me, not Mick, out there."

"Mick volunteered?" I didn't think he'd be that foolish.

"*Non*," Benoît shifts in his seat. "From the bank, we saw the two volunteers coming back. They'd chopped the key-logs and we knew the jam would explode." Benoît stares just over my head and I know he's back on the riverbank, reliving the moment. "Then I see someone else is still out there on the jam. It looks like his foot is caught. Before I can stop him, Mick is running, log to log, jumping across to the mountain of sticks. It could blow at any second."

My heart is racing. I see it, too.

"Taking the guy's cant-hook, Mick pries it under the log and frees him. They start running back and I see the guy was only a boy. The cook's boy. Trying to be the next Joe Montferrand tackling a jam." He shakes his head in disgust. "Jacques, he can't even split firewood right."

I swallow. "Jack?" I whisper, though I know before he nods.

"Just then, the jam exploded; timber flies into the air like matchsticks. Jacques, he got thrown clear, landed near the bank, bruised but alive. But there was no sign of Mick."

He pauses and clears his throat. I can only imagine the panic he must have felt, watching the dark river. Searching for a sign of Mick.

"The whole camp ran onto the rolling logs, looking for him in the rushing water. Every second counted. If Mick survived the blast, the logs would surely crush him or the freezing river would take him. But we found him." He turns his watery eyes to mine. "We found him."

The door clicks and Dr. Van Cortlandt comes out, untying his bloodied apron. "We've given him something for the pain. He's asleep now and he needs lots of rest," he says.

The news warms my heart more and more, as though a numb part of me has been pulled from icy depths.

"Still," he adds, slipping on his coat as Benoît stands, "he's not out of danger yet."

When the men leave, Sister Thibodeau rests her hands on my shoulder. "Your friend, he's a strong boy. I think he's going to make it."

"Can I see him?" I ask.

She nods.

He's sleeping under a pile of blankets, head bandaged. The blood has been washed from his face and arms. His skin is no longer a blue-gray. Though he's covered in cuts and stitches like a patched rag doll, he no longer looks like a butchered corpse. He looks like my Mick.

Sitting by the bed, I take his hand in mine. He doesn't stir. His calloused hands are as rough as the bark they'd been stripping. His arms and neck are thick and muscled. Whatever he'd been doing these long months, it suited him. The boy from Ireland, the inept sailor, my lanky brother, the awkward friend—none are the man I see before me.

I rest my fingers on his forearm, white and wrinkled from the burns he'd gotten the day we saved his mother, but my eyes are drawn to the newly healed scar just above it. I wonder how he got it. I wonder what has filled his life these past eight months?

I wonder if there is any space for me in it.

CHAPTER FIFTY

Day after day, I do my visits to the families in the morning and the sick in the afternoon. They move Mick into the room where Billy is, but still Mick hasn't woken up. He's breathing all right; his heart is strong; his color is good; and Sister Thibodeau says his wounds are healing well, no sign of infection. But whatever hit his head hit him hard. Be patient, Sister Thibodeau tells me. But how can I? What if he never wakes up? What if I've kept him from death only to have him live in that nothingness between awake and dreaming? The guilt of it weighs upon me.

And then one day, as I sit by him, spooning in drops of his broth and wiping his chin, Mick opens his eyes.

"Mick?" I set down the bowl and lean in.

"He's awake?" Billy asks from the other bed and pushes up on his good arm to see.

Mick's eyes try to focus as he frowns and looks at the room.

"Can you hear me, Mick?"

"Where … where am I?" His voice is hoarse and I pour a drink of water.

"You're at the hospital." I tilt the cup to his lips and set it back on the side table. "You were in an accident on the river."

He raises his hand to his head, and notices the bandage around it.

"You got a good clatter. Twenty stitches. Your side was badly damaged, too."

Lifting his head and wincing with the pain, he looks down at his side's black stitches, its purpled flesh, swollen, squished to near bursting between the bandages, like a plum in a vice.

"Dr. Van Cortlandt said it should heal well, though it may take a while."

"You've been out for nearly a week now," Billy says, from the other bed. "Not much of a roommate," he chides.

I rest my hand on Mick's; it makes him blush.

"I'm a bit confused," he says, rubbing his eyes. "So, I'm in the hospital?"

"In Bytown," I add. "God, 'tis good to see you, Mick." I squeeze his hand. "I've missed you so much."

"Give him some breathing air," Billy scolds. "He's barely awake."

I laugh. "I know, 'tis just I've so much to ask. So much to tell." I smile at Mick, but he doesn't smile back.

"I'm sorry," he says, frowning at me. "But do I ... do I know you, miss?"

Mick doesn't remember anything before the accident, not yet, anyway. Sister Thibodeau says that happens sometimes, but often something triggers the memories, cranks open the mind like the locks of the canal, and soon they come flooding back.

"So we were neighbors?" he asks, slurping his stew. His appetite is back, a good sign to be sure. I tell him then of our life in Killanamore, the rolling hills, the village, the people. I tell him of Lord Fraser and the Big House. I tell him of the time we kids battled like the Fianna, running wild on the hillside, how we hunted for lugworms and caught fish in the river; tell him of the day when Mam caught him and Jack throwing stones at the hen and how her look sent him bolting home like a jackrabbit.

"Sounds like I was a right scallywag!" He laughs.

When he asks, I tell him about his family. About his dead father, about how his mother and his two sisters, Meg and Nan, perished in the workhouse. I tell him how Kenny was killed working with my Da in England. His eyes fill with tears, for truly 'tis like losing them all over again.

"But you've an older brother in New York," I say. "Joseph."

Day after day, I pass him our tales of home, as though the breath of my memories will knock upon his heart and help him to find his own. I tell him all our stories, all but one. I never tell him how he loved me.

For if I have to tell him that, then surely he doesn't anymore.

Billy tells him stories, too. Old yarns every Irishman knows; well, every Irishman but Mick. I can hear them laughing as I go about my chores in the house. 'Tis the best medicine for them both. What a gift for Billy to find fresh ears for all those well-told tales. For even after Billy is healed and sent home, he comes back every couple of days to visit Mick.

Sister Thibodeau soaked Mick's shirt and pants in wood ash and soda to get rid of the blood stains. She patched and stitched them back together as painstakingly as she had Mick himself. "Here, Mick," she says, laying them on the foot of his bed one afternoon. "I thought you might like to get out of that sleeping shirt for a change, maybe even walk out on the stoop for a bit of air. Kathleen can help you."

His eyes light up; he's right eager to be free from the tiny room. Though I don't blame him. After all those long months in the woods, he must be getting antsy cooped up like this.

"Oh," she says, coming back into the room as I help him sit on the bed's edge to change into his clothes. "I forgot to give you this. I found it in your pocket." She hands him a small Celtic knot of braided straw. He studies it in his palm, deep in thought.

"A harvest knot," I whisper. I'd know that pattern anywhere, for I'd seen that tight weave, those interlacing loops once before. I'd found one just like it on my sitting stone back home. My heart tingles like thawing fingers. All this time, I thought that love knot was from Tom. I never realized Mick made it.

Mick looks up at me as though seeing me for the first time. His eyes widen and his mouth hangs open. Then, red-eared, he closes his fist and shoves the knot back into his pocket.

"Thanks anyway, Kit," he says, lying back down. "But I'm not feeling well. I think I'll have a rest instead."

Without another word, he turns his back to me.

I stand there for a moment, stunned, and then it dawns on me, slow and aching like the throb of chilblains.

He'd made that harvest knot in Ireland for me.

But who, who did he make this one for?

CHAPTER FIFTY-ONE

Mick isn't the same after that day. The harvest knot must have triggered a memory. The memory of her.

He no longer asks to hear stories of our days together, and when I try to tell one, he says he'd rather rest instead. 'Tis as though the very sight of me causes him pain. I can make neither head nor tail of it.

A hint of spring is in the air as winter melts and runs down gutters and muddy lanes. Everyone's spirits lift at the thought of better weather ahead, but not Mick's. And not mine.

I try to get him to come out. "The sun will do you good," I say. "You need to work your muscles."

But he won't listen to me. Only Billy or Benoît, on the days he stops by, can get him up and out for a bit.

Mick never speaks of remembering and I don't ask. Maybe I just don't want to know. It surprised me to think that he'd met a girl. Mick was never one for saying how he felt. But 'tis obvious he's pining for someone. Heartsick, it seems. Though, truth be told, I've caught a case of it myself.

How could he have met someone?

There aren't girls in the lumber camps, are there?

Did she live in a nearby town?

How serious can they be?

Serious enough to make her a love knot.

Serious enough to make him act like this.

Serious enough that he wants nothing to do with you.

My mind tosses like a ship at sea, lurching my stomach this way and that. I can't eat. I can't sleep. I can do nothing but wait.

I arrive at the hospital that afternoon and hang my cloak in the hall. I want nothing more than to be with Mick, but how many more times can I bear his shunning? He won't even look me in the eye. Even if he doesn't remember loving me, he surely can't forget the terrible way he's been treating me these past few weeks. I spoke to Mother Bruyere about it that morning, for she could tell I wasn't myself.

"Be honest," she'd said. "With him and with yourself."

She's right. As scary as it is, I've made up my mind to tell him the truth. To tell him I love him and let him know he loved me, once.

But when I round the corner, he's not there.

"He left with Billy and Benôit about an hour ago," Sister Thibodeau says. "Did they not tell you goodbye?"

Goodbye? What is she talking about?

"They're off to work on the lumber booms heading to Quebec."

"What?!"

She must be joking.

"They're taking the one o'clock steamer from Entrance Bay," she adds.

Without even stopping for my cloak, I bolt out the door and over Sussex to the shore, past where Martha and I once washed clothes. My breath rushes out of me in huffs as I splash through the puddles, covering my skirts in mud and slush. The wharf is empty except for Captain Baker, the postmaster, who stands on the quay sorting through two large sacks of mail bags hanging from his horse.

"The steamer," I pant. "Has it come?"

He takes in the state of me for a moment. "Uh, yes, miss. Gone about ten minutes ago."

I don't believe him. I can't.

Running back to the path's end at the base of the bluff, I enter the brush, yanking myself forward by stick and stump. Thorns slash my dirtied dress. My foot slips in the slushy mud and a branch cuts my cheek as I fall to my knees, but I keep going. Briars snag my bonnet. Ripping the ties, I leave it like a prayer rag on a rowan tree as I forge up the hill.

Please, God. Please, Mick. Please, God.

I have to reach the top. I have to see for myself.

Cresting the bluff, I tear from the brush and run to the edge. Log booms and lumber rafts float downriver like little towns. A few men stand on the edge of their rafts, navigating them to the lumberyards on the other side of the hill, while others continue on, winding their way past Bytown to towns beyond. I hear them calling to each other. Waving goodbye.

I raise my hand to the tiny curl of smoke on the horizon. To the steamer leaving. Maybe Mick will remember. Maybe he'll look back. Maybe he'll see me standing on the bluff and know I loved him.

CHAPTER FIFTY-TWO

"You'll catch your death of cold, and what good would you be then?" a voice says.

I spin around to see him sitting on the rock.

"Mick?" I can't believe it's him. "I thought ..." I glance at where the steamer disappeared. "Sister Thibodeau said you and Billy went with Benoît ..."

He shrugs and fiddles with the harvest knot in his thick, calloused fingers. "I couldn't leave."

"What are you doing here?" I finally say, walking over to him.

"I might ask you the same thing," he shakes his head. "Look at the state of you."

My dress is ripped, filthy with mud and wet from slush. Bits of my bun hang about my face in wet curls and my cheeks sting from where the branches cut. I'm a right mess. But none of that matters.

"I had to see … I thought you ..." Catching my breath, I feel the anger ignite in me. Hand on my hip, I point my finger at him. "Why didn't you tell me? After all I did for you … how could you leave me, just like that?"

He droops like a scolded pup.

"You're a right heartscald, Mick O'Toole. Do you know that?"

He looks up at me sideways. "B'jaysus, Kit, I swear you sound just like your mother. God rest her."

"Well, at least I—" the words catch in my throat. Awareness snuffs my anger. "You remember her? Mick? You remember my mother?"

He nods sheepishly.

"When did you start getting your memories back?" I wonder what else he remembers. I wonder if he remembers me.

"The day Sister Thibodeau gave me this." He hands me the harvest knot. "I made it in the shanty and kept it all this time."

I hold the knot in my shaking hands. "She must be special to you," I say, though my heart aches to even think it.

"She is," he admits.

And there it is. The truth of it. Mick is in love. But the words sadden him and his shoulders droop.

"I think she is promised to someone else," he adds.

Knowing Mick, he surely hasn't told the girl how he feels. Perhaps he has no chance with her. 'Twould be so simple to tell him to give up hope. But if anyone deserves happiness, 'tis Mick.

I hold out the knot. "You should give it to her, then."

He sticks his hands in his pockets and stares at the ground. "I just did."

My breath snags. I can't speak.

"Kit," he says, swallowing, steeling himself for the words to come. "I failed you. I tried my best to bring you Jack, but he wouldn't listen. I know having your family together is the most important thing to you … and I couldn't even do that. When the sister gave me this knot and I remembered, I remembered all I hadn't done for you. And the guilt of it ate me up inside. That's why I never told you I remembered."

I open my mouth to speak, to tell him I understand, to tell him

I'd let Annie go and that Jack deserved his freedom, too, but he puts his fingers lightly on my lips.

"Listen now, for I've only the nerve to say this the once. 'Tis one thing to long for you when I'm miles away in a lumber camp, for hope keeps me going. But to stand by you day after day and know that you'll never be mine?" He shakes his head. "Kit, I can't. I just can't. It kills me, so it does." He lowers his hands, slumping in defeat.

"You still love me, Mick?" I ask. I have to hear him say it.

"What does it matter?" He looks at me with tortured eyes. "If I couldn't win you away from that fool Tom Lynch, what hope have I against God Almighty?"

He won't say the words again. Won't nudge them out like a young robin fresh from the nest, only to see them dashed to the ground like they were in the storeroom of the ship those long months back. They perch in him, in both of us, teetering on the edge of flight. Or failure. I feel them battering their wings inside my heart.

Say it. Say it. Say it.

"Mick." I take a deep breath and let go. "I love you."

The words hang there for a moment between us. My stomach lurches with the sensation, as though I'm falling from a great height.

But Mick only stares at me, dumbfounded.

"I've always loved you," I continue. "I know I should have told you long ago, but I was scared." I swallow. "Like I only had so many pieces of my heart left to lose. But Mick, seeing you again, 'tis like … like a ..." I grasp for the words fluttering inside me.

"A knowing," he says, taking my hands again.

"Yes!" My heart soars, and despite my wet clothes and lack of a cloak, I feel as though I house a glowing coal. It radiates from my very core. "A knowing."

"Mick, whatever stories I've yet to live, I want to live them with you. Whatever epic battles lay ahead, I want you by my side. For as truly as I hold this knot, I feel, I *know* our souls are just as intertwined, woven together by God himself."

Mick moves closer and gently takes my face in his calloused hands. "So you're not a nun, then?"

"No," I whisper.

"Good," he says, as though he's afraid a bolt of lightning

might strike as he lowers his face to kiss me. But surely it does. It jolts our hearts as our lips meet, stirring up all those unspoken words. They flutter between us, around us, in a flock of heart whispers, making me dizzy.

I've no question where I belong. No doubt where my past and future lie. My heart has known my path all along, really. All it needed was time and the courage to fly.

A string of birds crosses the sky over Bytown. Spreading their wings, they glide and alight in the bay below, honking their arrival.

The geese are home. Finally home.

INTERVIEW WITH
CAROLINE PIGNAT

You were born in Ireland and lived there during part of your childhood, so your family did not participate directly in the migration you describe in Kit's story. Very briefly, what was it that made you want to tell this story?

I read the historical novel, *The Silent People* by Walter Macken, when I was sixteen and visiting Ireland. It tells the story of a famine in the 1700s. Having grown up in Canada, I did not know much about Irish history and I was amazed by the facts: families (indeed whole villages) starving to death, evictions, mass emigration, all because of a failed crop. They called it a "famine," but there was still plenty of food in Ireland – just not for the poor.

The Irish culture is known for its strong faith, quick humor, and generous hospitality, and I wondered how such people endured the reality of those harsh historical facts. I wondered, after all they'd endured in Ireland, how these people could find the strength and will to leave with nothing and start a new life in Canada.

Even though our immigration was nothing like theirs, I know what it is like to miss your homeland and your extended family. I know how it feels to be divided between two places. As someone who gets to go back and visit fairly often, I can only imagine how difficult it must have been for those early immigrants who had to leave their Irish homes, family and friends forever. In those days, the people in Ireland had wakes for people who left for they knew they'd never see them again.

I wrote an assignment in a grade eleven Writers Craft class over twenty years ago that was inspired by that summer's holiday in Ireland and reading of *The Silent People*. It is the seed of *Greener Grass*.

Research is a very important part of writing historical fiction. What was involved in doing the research necessary to write this book?

I read a lot of non-fiction about Irish history, the Great Famine, and the Irish culture. Thanks to a grant from the Canada Council for the Arts, I had the opportunity to tour many museums, famine exhibits, cemeteries, and historical and heritage centers in Ireland during 2006. I visited places such as: Muckross Farms, Skibbereen

Famine Museum, Abbestrewery Cemetery, Cobh Museum, National Museum of Farm Life, Wicklow Gaol; I took a day sail on the replica famine ship *Jeanie Johnston* and toured the *Dunbrody*.

Much of the story evolved as I researched. For example, it wasn't until I was touring Wicklow Gaol and saw the registry for "Child Inmates" from 1846-1850 that I realized children were stealing food and getting arrested for it. I knew then Kit had to commit a similar crime and meet many of these real life children.

I use binders to help me keep all my research organized. Okay, I obsess about them.

In telling your story, you have brought to life a number of real historical figures. What is the challenge to a writer in using real people in a work of fiction? Why did you choose to make use of them, rather than creating fictional characters in similar roles?

The challenge in using real people is to represent them as accurately as I can. Again, research is key. The historical figures like Captain McDonald, Father Robson, Dr. Douglas or Sister Thibodeau are minor characters in the story, but I wanted to accurately name them as a tribute to the important roles they played during that time in history

For more developed characters like Mother Bruyere, I had primary sources like her letters to give me a sense of her personality. I also had the archivist of the order read everything I wrote about Mother Bruyere. That was a condition of the archivist's assistance but it reassured me that I had caught the spirit of Mother Bruyere.

I chose to make my antagonists, Lynch and Lord Fraser, fictional, but based them on my research of many other landlords and middlemen of the time. That gave me the freedom to change their actions and personalities to suit my plot.

A few background characters (the Hyland family from Carrighill) were my mother's people whose names I discovered on a census from that period. Because I had nothing but their names to go on, I decided not to impose a personality and left them in the background, but I wanted them to be present.

In your story, while Kit wants to keep what remains of her family together, she fails; Jack sets off for the farms and lumbering trade of the Ottawa River, and Annie is adopted by a family who can give her a decent home. In your research, did you come across accounts of similar family breakups that occurred during this period?

Yes. The number of orphaned children really surprised me. Mother Bruyere runs an orphanage for young Irish children as well as St. Raphael's House for Irish teenage girls. Even at Grosse Isle, many children arrived as orphans. In one letter from Lord Elgin, he writes " … nearly 1,000 immigrant orphans have been left during the season at Montreal and a proportionate number at Grosse Isle, at Quebec, at Kingston, Toronto, and other towns." Father Cazeau himself found homes for 453 orphans. They often kept their Irish surnames; however many carried the typhus into their new families.

There are also advertisements in the local papers of the time of people trying to locate family members. The tragedy is that most of the poor Irish were illiterate.

One of the strengths of your story is the voice of Kit—the "lilt" of her telling, as Brian Doyle has called it. If you could name one person whose voice inspired this distinctive style, who would it be?

My mother.

According to your story, the Irish who came to Canada as a result of the potato famine and the disruption of their lives in the 1840s were treated badly when they arrived in Canada. Do you think this is also the way other immigrant groups have been regarded when they arrived here?

Yes. Though not all arrive in Canada with dire circumstances as those immigrants escaping wars, disasters, or exiles, I think people see immigrants as people arriving with "needs." Perhaps they need education, or health care, or employment; either way, the general public tends to react with stereotypes and prejudice, particularly if the group sticks to itself (Little Italy, Chinatown, etc.). If you add something like a contagious disease (typhus) or a job shortage, people are even more hostile to the newcomers. As people gain an understanding of the newcomers and their culture, they feel less threatened about what it's costing and more likely to see what that culture brings to the community. Ironically, it seems that the last group that experienced racism is okay with doing it to the newcomers. It reminds me of grade 10s making life hell for those "minor-niners."

In the fall of 2009, the first novel in which you tell the story of Kit and her family won a Governor General's Literary Award, the most prestigious prize for children's literature in Canada. How has that affected your life as a writer?

The award, like the Canada Council grants, is a great affirmation of my writing. To be so supported and recognized for literary excellence, particularly so early on in my career, makes me feel both honored and challenged.

What advice do you have for aspiring young writers?

I give them the same advice I continue to give myself: read lots and write lots. Keep learning the craft. Persevere and, most importantly, enjoy the ride.

AUTHOR'S NOTE

The summer of 1847 is known as the Summer of Sorrow. A tidal wave of Irish immigrants flooded Canadian shores. Thousands did not survive the journey. Thousands more succumbed to typhus and were buried at Grosse Isle. As the surviving immigrants moved inland, typhus traveled with them and many more Irish and Canadian people died. Yet the more I learned about the summer of 1847, the more it became a story of hope.

In times of tragedy, hope is found in one helping hand. Dr. Douglas, Father Robson, Father Cazeau, Mother Bruyere, Sister Thibodeau—these are just a few of the numerous Canadian men and women, the tireless heroes who dedicated themselves to the care of the Irish that summer. They reached out, showing extraordinary compassion and generosity, despite the dangers of disease. Soldiers, sailors, nurses, nuns, doctors, ministers, and priests, many, like Father Robson, lost their lives. But they did not lose hope. What a testimony of Canadian compassion. What an inspiration to the Irish.

Though some dates are modified to fit the plot (i.e., Dr. Benson died in May and Martha Hagan was already a nun by that summer), I have tried to weave in as much historical fact as possible.

THE CROSSING

Built in Quebec in 1845, the *Dunbrody*, like many ships of the time, served as a cargo ship carrying timber from Canada. Fitted with bunks for passengers, she carried Irish emigrants from New Ross to Quebec from 1845 to 1851. Crossing at the peak of the famine in the summer of 1847, she carried 313 passengers. The *Erin* and *Dunbrody* left New Ross for Quebec on April fourteenth, 1847. The journey took about six to eight weeks. Of the almost 100,000 people that sailed for Quebec in 1847, 5,282 died during the crossing and another 3,389 succumbed to illness once they arrived.

GROSSE ISLE

5,424 persons who, flying from pestilence and famine in Ireland,
in the year 1847, found in America, but a grave.

Inscription on the monument in the Irish Cemetery at Grosse
Isle.

Grosse Isle is an island in the St. Lawrence fifty kilometers
east from the port of Quebec. From 1832 to 1937 it served as a
quarantine station. The season of 1847 brought the greatest number
of immigrants to Grosse Isle, most of them Irish. Anchored for
days until space could be found on Grosse Isle, many healthy

passengers caught typhus and later died. Structures on the island were built to house 200 sick and 800 healthy passengers, but that year over 98,000 arrived. The priests and doctors mentioned in the novel were actual men who served on Grosse Isle. Doctor Benson was a passenger on the *Wandsworth* who offered his services upon reaching the island. Father Robson, known for his strength, often carried the sick right out of the hold on his shoulders when no one else would touch them. Like many other dedicated caregivers, Father Robson and Doctor Benson died from typhus that summer. Hundreds of children, like Annie, were left orphaned. Thanks to Father Cazeau and hundreds of Quebec families, over 450 Irish orphans were adopted that summer, many of whom kept their Irish surnames.

BYTOWN

Over three thousand Irish arrived in Bytown that summer, many with typhus. Their care fell to Mother Bruyere and her Sisters of Charity. Her letters to her Superior in Montreal show a woman of great faith and determination in the face of enormous need. Though she'd only arrived in Bytown two years before, Mother Bruyere (aged twenty-nine) and her small band of twenty-one women not only cared for the thousands of immigrants, but also opened hospitals, orphanages, schools, and Saint Raphael's Home. She was an integral part in the foundation of this small town that would one day become a nation's capital. For her decades of tireless work with women, the poor, and as a champion of health care and education, the Vatican is considering Mother Bruyere for beatification.

The Songs and Poems

"Shores of Amerikay" – Traditional

"The Flying Ships" by Thomas D'Arcy McGee from *The Poems of D'Arcy McGee With Copious Notes*, New York; Boston; Montreal: D.J. Sadlier, 1869.

ACKNOWLEDGEMENTS

Thanks so much to:

The Canada Council for the Arts, whose support allowed me the opportunity to thoroughly research this novel.

Peter Carver for being my North Star. Your guidance, affirmation, and brilliance not only keep me on track, but make the journey a joy. I look forward to our next adventures.

Richard Dionne, Lori Avakian, and the Red Deer Press crew for your continuous support and hard work.

Marie Campbell for your encouragement and navigating advice.

Alan Cranny, my father, for capturing the spirit of the story in the art of the cover and to Marion Pignat, my daughter, for your awesome photography.

Elizabeth Tevlin for your insightful feedback and wonderful humor.

Maureen Dufour for wise words in discernment.

Roger Chartrand for wild words in French.

To my family and friends who continue to support and inspire me in ways too many to mention. Thanks for being great traveling buddies.

We are blessed with faithful stewards of our past who share it so passionately with our future. You have all helped ensure that this novel rings true. A special thanks to experts in the field:

Sean Reidy and his knowledgeable *Dunbrody* crew in New Ross, Wexford. Sean, your hospitality is outdone only by your generosity and eagerness to share *Dunbrody*'s story. Thanks also to the staff of the replica famine ship, the *Jeanie Johnston*, for helping me sail into the past.

Israël Gamache of Grosse Isle and the Irish Memorial, Quebec. Israël, your passion for your work burns bright. Thanks for igniting it in others.

Authors Marianna O'Gallagher, Rose Masson Dompierre,

Andre Charbonneau, and Andre Sevigny for your detailed research of Grosse Isle.

Steve Dezort, Program Manager, Bytown Museum, for helping me unearth the history in my hometown.

Authors Sister Paul-Emilie, Emilien Lamirande, and Linda Fitzgibbon for your detailed accounts of Mother Bruyere and Bytown.

And a special thanks to Sister Louise Seguin of the Sisters of Charity. Your generosity with your time and knowledge was such a gift. Thank you for helping to bring Mother Bruyere and her companions to life in my heart.

A special thanks to:

Tony, Liam, and Marion. You make me laugh; you make me hope; you make me proud. You are what matters most. I love you guys.